**"What if I'm remembering his voice wrong?" she asked. "This whole ordeal has me questioning myself."**

"Your brain may have blocked out some details in order to protect you," he said. "The voice has been the one thing you've been clear on."

"What if I'm wrong?"

"Then that's okay too," he said. "You're trying to recover from something that had to be the scariest moment of your life. I believe you'll know if you hear him again. All you're trying to do is figure out who this perp might be."

"You're right," she said. She was being too hard on herself because she didn't want to give this perp the chance to strike again. "At least I won't be hiding any longer."

"No. You won't," he agreed. "I'll be right there, watching your back, making sure nothing bad happens. You're not alone any longer."

She blinked back tears. "You have no idea how much that means to me," she said. "And Atlas too. We both need you."

All my love to Brandon, Jacob and Tori, my three greatest loves. To Samantha for the bright shining light that you are. I love you more than words!

To Babe, my hero, for being my best friend, greatest love and my place to call home. I love you with everything that I am.

This book is dedicated to my sweet Shaq. Thirteen years is a long time to have you by my side. I can only hope we've given you the best possible life—a life you so richly deserve. Please run a little slower toward the Rainbow Bridge. I will miss you, my sweet boy.

# RESCUED BY
# THE RANCHER

—

*USA TODAY* Bestselling Author
# BARB HAN

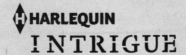

HARLEQUIN
INTRIGUE

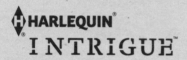

## INTRIGUE

ISBN-13: 978-1-335-58253-9

Rescued by the Rancher

Copyright © 2023 by Barb Han

Recycling programs
for this product may
not exist in your area.

Harlequin Enterprises ULC
22 Adelaide St. West, 41st Floor
Toronto, Ontario M5H 4E3, Canada
www.Harlequin.com

**Printed in U.S.A.**

*USA TODAY* bestselling author **Barb Han** lives in north Texas with her very own hero-worthy husband, three beautiful children, a spunky golden retriever/standard poodle mix and too many books in her to-read pile. In her downtime, she plays video games and spends much of her time on or around a basketball court. She loves interacting with readers and is grateful for their support. You can reach her at barbhan.com.

## Books by Barb Han

### Harlequin Intrigue

#### *The Cowboys of Cider Creek*

*Rescued by the Rancher*

#### *A Ree and Quint Novel*

*Undercover Couple*
*Newlywed Assignment*
*Eyewitness Man and Wife*
*Mission Honeymoon*

#### *An O'Connor Family Mystery*

*Texas Kidnapping*
*Texas Target*
*Texas Law*
*Texas Baby Conspiracy*
*Texas Stalker*
*Texas Abduction*

Visit the Author Profile page at Harlequin.com.

# CAST OF CHARACTERS

*Payton Reinert*—Can she escape a serial killer twice?

*Callum Hayes*—Will he leave his successful business to take his place at the family ranch, or will helping Payton escape a serial killer become his top priority?

*Masked Monster*—This serial killer won't rest until Payton is victim number six.

*Officer Wickham*—How much does he really know about this case?

*Nadine Humphrey*—This nurse is keeping a secret. Is she the key to finding the killer?

# Chapter One

It had started with a bad feeling. The kind that sat heavy on the chest while sending prickly sensations up the spine. Some people called it intuition. Others described it as a sixth sense, a warning of danger ahead. To this day, Payton Reinert questioned why she hadn't listened to that little voice in the back of her mind telling her to be cautious. Maybe it was his politeness that had slipped through her defenses. Or the fact that she'd been flustered and in a hurry. She hadn't wanted to make two trips from the car with the heavy plastic bags of groceries. So, she'd tried to bring up all five at once, balancing the plastic straps on her arm as they left deep grooves on her skin. It would all be worth it once she got inside and kicked off her boots.

Payton had done this same routine before when she was tired and couldn't wait to get off her feet after a long shift at the coffee shop followed by hoofing it around campus. Grad students didn't need a gym pass after all that walking to get to classes, plus all the stair climbing in the crowded old buildings at the

University of Texas at Austin. The barista job might cause her to wake up in the middle of the night, but the hours were easy to work around her class schedule. Plus, she didn't mind going to bed early. Her great-aunt had always teased that Payton had missed her calling, saying she could have been a great farmer with the hours she kept.

There was something about taking a break to watch the sun rise every morning that fed her soul. She'd been in too big a hurry this morning to do that, too. So many missed steps that led to this point.

The door to her building had a stick at the bottom, ensuring it didn't close or lock. She couldn't count the number of times she'd gotten on her neighbors in 2B about leaving the security door ajar. How hard was it to walk downstairs when they were having a party, which, by the way, seemed like every night? Chase Wilson had promised to stop, but there the stick was, wedging the door open. At least it benefited Payton today, so she didn't have to dig around for her keys. Considering it was the weekend before Halloween, she should have expected Chase to pull a stunt like this one.

Payton kicked the stick away from the door after throwing her shoulder into it, muttering a curse. Navigating the stairs while carrying what felt like her weight in groceries, she knew what it felt like to be an ant.

The bag with all the canned goods ripped halfway up, sending its contents tumbling down with a loud thud. Payton cursed loudly this time.

"Don't worry about it, I'll grab them." The unfamiliar male voice came from around the corner at the bottom of the stairwell, along with a little niggle of discomfort. Didn't she know everyone in the building?

"No, it's okay. I can make a trip down," she said, thinking that of course this happened today. She'd almost creamed someone on the way home when they turned right on a red without checking first. Her blood pressure was still through the roof from that.

The guy had a nice enough voice and was being polite, as he was practically on all fours rounding up the cans. Did she really want to make the trip downstairs only to reclimb those same steps?

"It's fine. Really. I'm running late, so I don't have a lot of time, but this is nothing. It'll only take a second," he continued without looking up. He was in some type of costume, something furry, which meant he was probably arriving early for yet another of Chase's parties.

When the guy stood up, arms filled with soup and vegetable cans, she got a full view of what he was wearing. Apparently, she was dealing with the beast from *Beauty and the Beast*.

A voice in the back of her mind told her not to comment.

"I'm guessing my neighbor is having another party tonight, based on your getup," she conceded.

"Yeah, Chase," he said as he took the stairs two at a clip. He looked at the load she was carrying, and then the bluest eyes caught her gaze—a disarming shade. On instinct, she took a step back but she wouldn't have been able to explain why even if someone had asked her.

"I can take one of those." He motioned toward the bags. A few wisps of thick, curly black hair peeked out of the mask.

"No, thanks," she said.

He took a step forward and said, "Really, it's no trouble."

He extended his hand and stepped closer.

Payton ignored the tension mounting in her shoulders, writing it off as a bad day. This guy was being friendly and polite. All he wanted to do was help her carry her groceries upstairs.

"What's your floor?" he asked, expectantly.

"I'm on three." Payton handed over a couple of bags.

"Then it won't take long to get these inside so I can be on my way," he said, and she could almost feel his smile through his mask.

"Right," she said before turning and walking up the next flight. She stopped in front of her door and turned around as she reached one hand inside her purse for the keys. "I can take it from here."

He made a show of juggling the cans in his arms.

"Prop the door open if you want, but it'll only take a second for me to run in and drop these on the counter," he said. "I'll even be the one to close the door on the way out if it makes you feel better."

There was something in his tone that made her feel silly for not trusting him. Still. Something was still niggling at the back of her mind.

Against her better judgment, she nodded.

Payton turned around and unlocked the door.

"Okay, but keep it open," she said as she entered the apartment. "And ignore the mess."

"I promise," he said a few seconds before she heard the door click closed.

Halfway across the room already, Payton turned around to protest and was startled by the man, who was right behind her with a gun in his hand that was pointed at the center of her chest.

"Yell and you're dead," he said.

"I won't," she responded despite the shock taking hold. Her mistakes clicked into place, and she realized just how much trouble she was in.

"Which way to the bedroom?" he asked.

She pointed to the hallway off the kitchen.

"Show me," he practically ordered. His voice was a spine-chilling mix of stress, adrenaline and triumph.

A sick feeling overtook Payton as bile burned the back of her throat.

"Take off your pants and get on the bed," he ordered.

"Okay," she said as fear reverberated through her. She didn't dare look away or blink. Doing everything he asked might keep her alive. So she removed her pants.

"Stay right here," he said. "I need to get something from the kitchen."

"Okay," she said as he walked over and closed the window. The strange thing about his demeanor was that it was suddenly casual now.

He walked out of the room, stopping long enough to turn on the TV and crank up the volume. In that moment, it clicked. If she stayed there, she would be dead. Jumping into action, she grabbed the throw blanket from on top of her bed and then wrapped it around her midsection.

Rustling came from the kitchen—it sounded like he was rummaging through the drawers. Was he looking for a knife? Yes, she decided. The gun had been meant to scare her and gain her cooperation, but a shot would draw attention. A knife would be quiet. Besides, he probably assumed she wouldn't even scream at this point if he told her not to. She'd followed enough of his commands for him to relax. He had her, and he knew it.

Except the bastard was wrong.

With the TV creating a noisy distraction and his back turned, Payton slipped past the kitchen and right out the door. She bolted down the stairs to Chase's apartment, guessing his door would be unlocked. She gripped the door handle while saying a silent prayer it would open when she twisted the knob.

It did. She bolted inside, closed and locked the door behind her, and then turned around to a stunned-looking Chase with his buddy sitting on the sofa playing video games. Chase's mouth fell open at the sight of her.

"Call 911," she said as her body began to tremble. "Please. Right now. Someone is in my apartment. I was almost raped."

"Oh hell," Chase said, wide-eyed and with shock

in his voice. He picked up the cell phone on the coffee table in front of him before jumping to his feet.

With her back flat against the door, Payton slid down to her bottom. Her heart battered the inside of her rib cage. She was alive. She'd made it. She was safe.

"I HEAR THERE'S a new resident across the street," Callum Hayes said to his mother as they stood in the kitchen of his childhood home in Cider Creek, Texas. Other than his grandfather's funeral last month, Callum hadn't been here in years. Neutral territory had been his mantra when it came to his relationship with Duncan Hayes. Now? The regrets could be crippling if Callum focused on them. Since his grandfather was gone from a sudden heart attack while working the cattle and there was no going back to fix the past, there was also no use beating himself up over it again.

"How'd you hear about that?" his mother, Marla, asked.

"Stopped off for gas once I got to town," he said. "You know how folks like to talk."

"Moved in a week ago. Keeps to herself, though," his mother said on a shrug. She was all of five feet two inches with kind eyes and a warmth most people were drawn to. The saying about opposites attracting was certainly true in his parents' case. They'd made it work for them, too, considering they were married for decades before his father died in a car crash when Callum was still in high school. His parents had been high school sweethearts who'd started dating at sixteen years old and never stopped.

"Some folks move to the country for more privacy," he said. "Has anyone gone over to introduce themselves and try to get to know her?"

"She's only been here a week," his mother said. "Figured I'd let her settle in first."

His mother had been acting strange recently, and this was further proof. Losing her father-in-law and being given the responsibility of the ranch seemed to be wearing on her.

"Since when have you ever worried about letting the dust settle before you made someone feel welcome?" He cocked an eyebrow.

"I'm just happy that you came home," she responded. He wished he could say the same. This was probably the time to tell her not to expect a moving truck to pull up in front.

He studied his mother for a long moment before responding.

"Are you sleeping?" he asked, noticing the bags underneath her eyes despite her attempt to hide them with makeup.

"Enough, I guess," she said on a shrug. "How about a cup of coffee?"

He noticed how quickly she'd changed the subject after artfully dodging giving a real answer.

"I can get it," he said, but she was already on her way to the pot of fresh brew.

"Let me spoil you the first day, at least," she said, waving him off.

Callum knew when he'd lost an argument, and this was one of those times. So, he took a seat on a stool tucked under the lip of the granite island. "How's Granny?"

"She's doing better," she said before pouring two cups and then setting one down in front of him. "You still take yours black, right?"

"Yes, ma'am," he said. "Thank you for this." He lifted his mug in salute.

His mother raised hers to the same height before taking a sip after blowing to cool the drink. She'd asked him to come home to take his rightful place at Hayes Cattle, a multimillion-dollar ranching operation. Now that his grandfather was gone, the place was too big for one person to run successfully. A business owner himself, he figured there had to be other options besides the grandchildren coming home.

"What about your brothers and sisters?" she asked. "When should I expect them?"

"We haven't even finished our first cup of coffee and we're already talking shop." He'd arranged to be away from work to be with his mother for a couple of weeks while he cleared up the fact that he had a life in Houston, not Cider Creek. He figured he'd be able to slip out of town and back to his successful logistics business in a couple of weeks once he helped his mother find a better alternative. As it so happened, cattle ranching had taught him a thing or two about moving product from one place to another. Logistics was just that—making sure a company's goods made it from production warehouse to retailers. He'd done quite well for himself. The sense of pride that came with the fact he'd made his own way in life was irreplaceable. He didn't need Hayes money or the ranching life, despite how much he loved the land. He'd done well on his own terms after his grandfather warned Callum would be nothing without the family business.

"I'm anxious to get all my children under one roof," she said, holding on to the mug with both hands. Callum took note of the fact she didn't make eye contact when she responded. All of his siblings had wondered what their mother was up to when he'd warned them about her request for them to come home and take their rightful places at the ranch.

Don't get him wrong, he loved the land, and there was something very right about being back here. He'd never ached for home until walking through the front door ten minutes ago. And now the feeling had lodged itself in his chest, burrowing like a red fox. Still, he had a life in Houston.

"Do I hear one of my boys in here?" Granny's voice boomed from the hallway.

"It's me. Callum," he said in case she expected someone else or her memory was beginning to slip. He'd been preparing himself for every scenario on the drive over. One involved a dire medical diagnosis with his mother. Other than being tired, she didn't appear to be sick. Another included his granny receiving bad health news.

She practically skipped into the room.

"Callum Hayes." She stopped long enough to make

a show of rubbing her eyes. "Is that my eldest grandson home to stay?"

"It's me," he admitted, but that was as far as he planned to go today. He'd figured he would get in for a couple of days and assess the situation at home. His brothers and sisters were waiting on word as to whether or not they needed to make arrangements to cover their businesses and jobs so they could head home. Callum figured it shouldn't take too long to get the lay of the land, and it seemed senseless for everyone to descend on the ranch for a false alarm. His mother had been clear at the funeral a few weeks ago that she was perfectly capable of running things. She'd instructed her children not to worry. They didn't, because she was still young, not yet sixty five years old, and her mind was sharp as a tack. This year she'd forgotten a couple of birthdays, but who didn't slip every now and then?

Had it been a sign of something else brewing? Tension corded his muscles thinking about the possibility of losing his mother. Before he could get too far down that line of thinking, Granny made a bee-line for him and then wrapped her arms around his midsection. She was the same height as her daughter.

"I was beginning to think you'd never come home again," Granny said, a slight accusatory note in her voice. She'd never been one to keep her opinions to herself.

"I'm here now," he said. "How about joining us for coffee?"

"I believe I'll have a cup to celebrate," Granny

said. She started to wag her finger at Callum, which meant she was about to fuss at him again.

"Did you make your famous muffins?" He motioned toward the basket on the island.

Granny's face broke into a wide smile as she nodded.

"Mind if I take a couple of those?" he asked, thinking he needed an excuse to step out of the kitchen and what was shaping up to be a squall. Normally, he'd take two-to-one odds and have no trouble betting on himself. His mother and granny were formidable when they teamed up, and he could sense the shift taking place. They were about to hit him with questions he didn't have answers to, and he'd never been a good liar, so he didn't even try.

"Help yourself," Granny said. "I baked them for you."

"Mind if I share them instead?" he asked, thinking now was as good a time as any to introduce himself to the new neighbor.

"Suit yourself." Granny's eyebrow shot up.

"I'll be back in a few minutes," he said.

"You just got here," his mother protested, but there was no conviction in her tone. He wasn't the only one good at figuring out when a battle was lost before it began.

Callum drained his coffee mug, picked up the muffin basket and smiled.

"This shouldn't take long," he said.

"All right," his mother conceded. "When you get home, I'd like to sit down and talk."

"You'll have my full attention," he said, concerned at the sound of his mother's words. She looked healthy. Granny seemed just as spry as ever. Maybe Marla had realized handling ranch business on her own was too much for one person. Or maybe the worst case was true and more bad news was coming.

Callum's muscles tensed at the possibility of losing his mother, too. He shoved the thought aside, unable to fathom becoming an orphan.

Besides, his curiosity was growing about the mystery neighbor across the street, and he wanted to know why she was being so secretive. There was only one way to find out, and he hoped he wouldn't regret barging in on someone who didn't seem to want to be disturbed.

## Chapter Two

Callum parked beside the main house that looked in desperate need of repair. There were lights on in the barn, so he headed there with his basket of goodies, hoping to find the town's new resident and not startle her in the process. The place hadn't been lived in for at least a couple of years, possibly more, and it showed.

Music drifted out of the barn. He recognized the song as "The Loft" by successful country singer Raleigh Perry. At least the new resident had good taste in music.

The light tap at the door must not have broken through the volume, since there was no response, so he popped his head inside the door. Rapid-fire barking preceded the scariest, angriest dog he'd ever seen lunging toward Callum. Cujo lunged, but his leash stopped him cold. Long, sharp teeth snapped at Callum.

"Atlas. No!" a female voice boomed from the back of the barn. A woman came running toward the animal. Her gaze shifted to Callum, and pure fear crossed over her features. She had long, straight dark brown hair with caramel highlights and bangs that rested just above long, black eyelashes. She was taller than average and all legs.

"I'm your neighbor. Callum Hayes," he shouted over the barking. "My mother is Marla Hayes." The names seemed to resonate. Unexpected drop-ins had always been welcomed in Cider Creek. Most new folks were eager to meet the people who lived around them, since there was usually a family connection involved as the reason someone new moved here. But this stranger looked ready to jump out of her skin.

"I brought muffins," he said, holding up the basket and feeling mighty stupid for the intrusion. "I can just drop them off and go." He had no idea if she could even hear him over Atlas. The dog looked like an Akita mix, not something to be messed with.

"He's not friendly," she shouted before scrunching up her face as she took the leash in both hands. She tried to tug the hundred-pound animal backward. She planted both of her feet and leaned all her weight, but the dog was much stronger. There was a bag of treats sitting on a barrel next to her. She managed to grab one and toss it right in front of Atlas's nose, distracting him.

Callum was half-surprised when she followed him outside. Once they were out of the animal's view, Atlas quieted.

"He's a rescue," she said by way of explanation. "A project."

"A dog like that requires a lot of patience," Callum said. "You probably already know this, but tread lightly until you figure out what triggers him."

"He doesn't like men," she stated before offering a handshake. "I'm Payton, by the way. My aunt said a lot of good things about your family."

"Don't believe half of it," he joked, taking the offering. The zing of electricity at physical contact was as unwelcome as an ice storm in Texas. His heart was just as unprepared.

Payton stared down at their hands for a second longer than normal, giving him the impression she'd had the same reaction. At least he wasn't the only one. She quickly took her hand back, and he realized they'd both held on longer than necessary. He chalked it up to being caught off guard by an attraction—or whatever it was happening between them—because the air crackled with electricity.

The fearful look returned to her eyes, and that was the equivalent of a bucket of ice water being poured over his head.

"My grandmother made these muffins as a sort of welcome to the neighborhood for you combined with a welcome home for me." He handed over the assortment of blueberry, banana nut, and chocolate chip muffins.

Payton scanned the area as she took the basket. Strange behavior unless she was scared of someone or something being in the tree line.

"Thank you," she said, finally meeting his gaze. Another zing of electricity shot through him when their eyes met.

He ignored it, cleared his throat, and said, "My pleasure."

"You mentioned a homecoming," she said. Her rapid breathing and tense posture said she was working very hard not to bolt.

"Of sorts," he stated, not sure how much of his own story he wanted to get into. His curiosity about hers was racking up. Call it boredom or the nagging guilt of knowing he was about to let his mother down when he explained his life was in Houston and not here at some point during his trip home, but he was looking for an excuse to hang around. Maybe giving up a little information about himself would help Payton trust him enough to open up a little. "My grandfather passed away recently."

"I'm so sorry for your loss," Payton said. The sincerity in her tone was more comforting that it should be coming from a stranger.

"Thank you," he responded. "I really mean that."

She nodded, and some of the fear in her brown eyes was replaced with warmth.

"My mother asked me and my siblings to come home," he continued. "Said she needs to speak to us about taking up our rightful places on the family cattle ranch but I think there might be more to it."

She studied him.

"Except you don't want to," came the astute observation.

"Not particularly. No," he admitted.

"Mind if I ask why?" she continued.

"I built a successful business in Houston. My siblings have done the same in their lives, either starting their own businesses from scratch or taking a job they felt called to do. Heck, I don't even know what one of my brothers does since he left the military but the point is that he chose to do it," he explained. "Our mother has always been strong and confident. After our grandfather passed, she told us not to worry about the ranch because she was fully equipped to run the place on her own. Now, she seems to be backtracking."

"I'm guessing you're wondering why the sudden change of heart," she surmised.

"Exactly," he said, noticing how easy conversation was with Payton. Callum wasn't normally the talkative type.

"Is everything okay with her health?" she asked.

"I'm not sure yet. I hope so. She looks good, healthy," he said. "The last few weeks have been hard on her. She was as close to my grandfather as anyone could have been."

"What about your father?" she asked.

"He died years ago while I was in high school. My parents married right out of high school."

"I can't even imagine people being together that long," she said, and there was a wistful quality to her voice.

This didn't seem like the time or place to bring up the fact he'd believed he'd found his forever partner once not all that long ago. Finding her in bed with his friend had helped him see the reason she kept putting off getting married after dating for five years.

"It boggles the mind. I think they just got lucky," he said on a shrug. He'd taken happy marriages for granted after growing up with his parents. They made it seem like the most normal thing to find a life partner, marry, and bring up a family.

Callum had never been in a rush, but he'd truly believed his relationship with Hannah had been the real deal. So much for his judgment when it came to matters involving the opposite sex. He'd been determined to strike out on his own and make his way in life. The wife and family were supposed to fall into place after. At forty-two and with a failed relationship under his belt, along with no desire to jump right back on the horse, he was starting to think the ship had sailed.

"Happily-ever-after isn't for everybody," he said out loud before he could reel the words back in. Words like those invited questions—questions he could already see dancing in Payton's eyes.

"What brings you here?" Callum asked. At over six feet tall, with solidly muscled arms and a body built for sin, Callum Hayes fell into the category of Seriously Gorgeous Men. He had dark hair that was not quite brown and hinted at a Scottish-Irish heritage with natural reddish-blond highlights.

"I inherited this place when my great-aunt passed away a while back and figured it was time to fix it up to sell it," she managed to say without sounding like a complete idiot while coming up with an on-the-spot excuse for her timing. "Do you mind if I check your ID?"

The question netted quite the look, but she needed to be certain this guy was who he said he was. He produced his wallet and then ID. It checked out, and she was grateful he didn't ask why she wanted to see it. Adopting a dog from a shelter on her way out of Austin and now hiding out in her aunt's house until her attacker was caught wasn't something she wanted to share. After the attack a week ago, she hadn't been able to imagine feeling this at ease in any man's presence. She had a long way to go before she'd be comfortable, but this was a starting place, and she had no desire to push the issue. Still, she was living alone in a town she didn't know. It might be nice to have someone to be able to call on in an emergency, and Callum had said that he lived across the street. Temporarily, at least.

"You're probably right about the happily-ever-after bit," she conceded, wondering who had burned him into embracing the idea. A guy as hot as Callum would have women lined up for the opportunity to spend time with him. From their conversation so far, she'd gleaned that he'd started and run a successful business. He was intelligent. And he had to be kind, or he wouldn't have brought over the basket. Speaking of which, she asked, "Do you want to come inside for a cup of coffee and a muffin?"

"Sure," he said. "Will Cujo be all right in the barn?"

"You mean Atlas?" she asked before realizing he was making a joke. Under normal circumstances, it would be funny. After the attack, she'd lost a lot of things. Her sense of humor was one of them. She forced a smile. "I'll get him if you grab this." She held up the basket that smelled amazing. "And I'll have to give you my key." She fished it out of her pocket after handing over the goodies.

His eyebrow shot up at the mention of a key, and she remembered folks in these parts didn't lock anything up. She'd already asked for his ID, which probably sounded strange enough.

"I'm from Austin," she said by way of explanation, hoping he would leave it at that. She dropped the key in his open palm, unwilling to risk physical contact again after the way electric impulses had reverberated through her from the handshake. She'd never felt so much intensity from one touch before, and it both scared and intrigued her.

"Got it," he said. Those two words were loaded, but he seemed content with not asking for an explanation.

"Go ahead on in and wait in the kitchen. Excuse the mess, though. I'll be right there." Payton decided it might be nice to have a friend here in Cider Creek, and her great-aunt had spoken highly of her neighbors. Payton almost wished she'd spent summers here instead of being bounced back and forth between parents, who'd been more interested in using her as a weapon and then a babysitter. She'd spent her young years in Dallas. Both parents had remarried and had other children, whom she'd been given responsibility of babysitting from early on. She'd moved to Austin to go to college and never looked back, working jobs while taking classes as she could afford to. Thinking back to how relieved her parents had seemed the first year she'd told them she wouldn't be able to come home for a holiday made her relive the disappointment all over again despite the fact she was into her thirties and should probably be over the rejection by now.

Since she didn't need to be reminded of how little they cared about her or her welfare, she'd taken it as a sign and moved on from their lives. Other than the annual birthday wish on social media, her mother never reached out. Her father had moved on long ago with his new wife and sons.

She forced her gaze away from Callum as he entered her home through the squeaky screen door on the back porch. There wasn't much quiet about her great-aunt's home—the place was in need of many repairs. Even so, the inheritance was a godsend now.

Payton hadn't been able to bring herself to come here after learning of her great-aunt's passing a couple of years ago. Now, it was the perfect place to lie low until the man in the beast mask could be caught.

Atlas jumped to his feet the second she walked inside the barn. His tail wagged. None of the aggression she'd witnessed toward Callum was present in Atlas's demeanor now. The shelter had warned her about Atlas and strange men when she'd picked him out from the line of cages. In that instant, she'd known he was going home with her.

After what happened, she wasn't a fan of strangers, either. And she'd made a vow never to be caught off guard or go against her instincts again.

It hadn't taken long to explain to her graduate professors what had happened and get their approval to finish out her semester online. She had no idea what she was going to do about next semester. She was too close to graduation and her master's in social work to quit, but she doubted she could go back to Austin to live.

And then there was her job at the coffee shop. It might not have been much, but she'd made enough to cover classes and keep a roof over her head. Now, she would have to figure out another way to make ends meet.

She could use the money she'd saved for next semester to live on, take a semester off to get back on her feet and figure out a plan. Maybe she could ask Callum about possible job opportunities in Cider Creek. Possibly something that wouldn't have her dealing directly with the public. Night stocker at the grocery store came to mind. Or stall cleaner. She could tolerate animals better than people right now.

Except when it came to Callum. There was something different about him. And even though there was no way she could trust another human right now, talking to him had a surprisingly calming effect on her.

Leaning into it would be a mistake. Keeping him at arm's length would be no problem with what she'd just been through. And yet, her heart warned her to keep a safe distance from this man. Could she?

## Chapter Three

The inside of the widow Beverly Baker's former home was as in much need of repair as the exterior. The past couple years of neglect showed through in the need for paint inside and out, the overgrown grass that threatened to overtake the landscape, and the long stretches of fence in need of reinforcement and a good coat of stain. There was clearly no way to let Atlas go outside on his own to relieve himself.

Surprisingly, all the original furniture was still here, albeit moved around. A dresser blocked the front door, and a temporary bed had been set up in the living room. The place looked barricaded, causing him to worry for her safety. Was there an ex-boyfriend in the picture somewhere? Ex-husband? Ex-lover? The fact she'd asked for his ID gave him all kinds of questions. Why did she need to check to see he was who he said? Had a stranger caused her to be afraid of new people?

Those other labels, the intimate ones, made Callum more uncomfortable than they should with someone he'd met an hour ago. He rummaged around the kitchen long enough to find everything necessary to fix a pot of coffee.

As the pot started the first drip, Payton walked in the back door. Atlas was still on the leash and pulling hard enough to rip Payton's arm out of its socket. The dog started rapid-fire barking the minute he realized Callum was there.

Atlas was another clue Payton was hiding from someone. Since she'd gotten a dog that was afraid of men, it wasn't difficult to put two and two together.

"Might want to give him a treat to get him to calm down," Callum suggested, but the dog was too upset.

"I'll let him stay on the back porch for a while," she said, walking him out the back door. She returned a few seconds after Atlas calmed down.

"Things look different from the last time I was here," he said to her as the last of the coffee dripped into the pot. But that was a long time ago.

"Yeah," she said on a sigh. "I guess so." She started pacing. "I can only imagine what you must be thinking."

He held up a hand to stop her as he watched tension rise.

"You don't owe me any explanations," he stated.

Payton didn't immediately respond, so he moved forward with filling their mugs with coffee. He needed to get back across the street soon. He'd head back after the coffee.

Callum handed over a mug. Their fingers grazed, causing electrical impulses to tingle in his hand and reverberate up his arm. He stretched out his arm to shake it off.

"This place, the furniture arrangements, and the fact I showed up out of the blue must look suspicious," she said to him, motioning toward the wooden table that centered the room.

He took a seat and she followed.

"Something happened in Austin, where I live alone," she began. The rim of her coffee mug became very important. "*Lived*, I should say."

"I'm guessing it's the reason you showed up here," he said, pointing out the obvious, but it was a way to get her talking more. Her story might not be any of his business, but he wanted to offer help if he could.

"And why I picked up the dog at the shelter as well as moved the dresser so there was only one entrance," she admitted, and her cheeks turned a darker shade of red. Was she embarrassed? "This behavior might seem extreme, but I was nearly…"

She flashed her eyes at him, and he realized what she was trying to say. Raped, murdered or both.

"This person…was it someone you knew?" he asked.

"The police said I might know him or that he could have been watching me for a while," she explained. "He had on a Halloween mask from *Beauty and the Beast*, so I could probably pass him in the street and not know who he was." Her body shivered. "Except his eyes. I'll never forget those. They're burned into my brain." She brought her hands up to her forehead.

"Does that mean he's still out there, running around free?" he asked.

"I'm afraid so," she said. "And I know exactly what he planned to do to me, because he's done it before. There have been five others." She looked up for a second before going back to studying the rim of her coffee mug. "No survivors other than me."

"The bastard needs to be locked behind bars for the rest of his life," Callum ground out.

"You won't get any argument from me there," Payton said. "Until they catch him, I decided to move here. I've been needing to fix the place up and think about selling it anyway. I just couldn't fathom parting with it right after my great-aunt passed away. This was all I had left of her." She flexed and released her fingers a few times in what he assumed was an attempt to rein in her emotions. Callum knew all about holding it all in until he felt like he might explode.

"I'm here for a few weeks," he said. "I'd be happy to help out with whatever needs done. I'm actually pretty handy with a hammer."

"You have enough on your plate with your family," she argued, but there wasn't a whole lot of conviction in her voice.

"Nothing a few conversations can't fix there," he explained. "The main reason I decided to stick around for a few weeks is to make sure my mother is actually okay and not hiding something. She has been cryptic with me, and that's not like her. Then again, she's been off in general and I can't quite put my finger on it."

"It's understandable," Payton said with sympathy.

"Either way, I'll be there for her," he said. "And I'll still have time to help out a neighbor. It's a way of life in the ranching community."

"Austin used to be home to me. But, honestly, I lived in the same building with people I never got to know beyond an occasional nod or *good morning*. The only reason I know one of my neighbors is because I had to introduce myself so I could politely ask him not to wedge the security door open or party so loudly on a weeknight," she said, holding tight to her coffee mug. "The thought of going back to pack up my things and move them into storage until this place is ready..." She shivered as she spoke.

"I own a logistics company. We move products from one place to the next using trucks and trains. If you give me your address, I can have your things boxed up and in storage in a blink."

"I don't know. That's asking a whole lot, and—"

"It's literally nothing. I can have it done before your head hits the pillow tonight," he said.

She tilted her head to one side as her gaze unfocused, like she was looking inside herself for the right response.

"Please, it'll make me feel useful," he continued.

"Actually...that would be amazing," she said. "But how will they get in without a key?"

"How about your landlord? You give him or her a call or shoot a text, and we'll take care of the rest," he said. "Speaking of safety, getting a security system installed here wouldn't hurt. In the meantime, you can use one of those door cameras."

"I'm not sure how long I'll be living here," she hedged, but he thought there might be more to the story. She fished out her phone and made a quick call, letting her landlord know the plan.

"Atlas is good security," Callum pointed out after getting her address and landlord's information, then sending a text to Gregory Brewer back at the office. "No one will be able to sneak up on you as long as he's in the room."

"I keep a shotgun by the door, too," she said, but the uncertainty in her voice told him she didn't know how to use it.

He nodded, thinking she wouldn't hesitate to shoot after what she'd been through, and her choice of weapon was good for someone with little to no experience.

"This shouldn't have happened to you," he said quietly, trying to contain the slow-burning anger at the thought of the bastard who'd tried to hurt Payton being able to run free and prey on others.

"The whole thing is awful on so many levels," she admitted with a look that pierced his chest. "I hate how I'm afraid of my own shadow now, even though I'm determined not to let fear run my life. I hate how I had to drop everything I knew and run, as though I'm somehow the bad guy. And I hate that I wasn't able to stop him before he might do this to someone else, someone who might not be as lucky as I was."

"Luck is one way to describe it, but after meeting you, it sells you short," he said.

"How so?" Her eyebrows drew together like he'd confused her with the statement.

"You're brave and determined, and my guess is that's why you're sitting here at the table with me today rather than what could have happened," he pointed out. She needed to know how incredible and brave she was, and he wanted to be the one to tell her, for reasons that didn't need examining.

"I just wish I could feel safe again for five minutes," she said on a sharp sigh. "But thank you for the compliments."

An idea came to him, but he had no idea how she would respond. There was only one way to find out.

"You're welcome to stay at the ranch while you fix this place up," he said, then didn't realize he held his breath while waiting for an answer.

PAYTON SUPPRESSED A gasp at the offer. Could she really consider staying at the ranch across the street with Callum?

"Before you decide, let me provide context," he continued. "The main house is huge. There are eight bedrooms, plus a guest suite on the first floor."

Her mouth almost dropped to the ground. The home wasn't visible from the street and the drive was protected by a gate, she'd noticed immediately as she'd driven past. Her great-aunt had mentioned the house across the street looked like it belonged in its own zip code. Beverly had inherited her home from her father. The place had been passed down four generations. Land had been parceled out and sold, so there was a small development on this side of the street.

"Right now, there's only three of us living in the main house," he continued without missing a beat. "So, we're literally rattling around in the big house full of empty rooms."

The idea held a whole lot of appeal. Except she was neglecting to consider one very important thing... Atlas.

"I can't," she said, her shoulders deflating. "I have someone else to think about besides myself, and it wouldn't be fair to Atlas."

"The best way to train a dog is with other dogs," he stated. "Unless he's aggressive with them. Then, there isn't much that can be done unless I volunteer to stay here with you."

"He won't allow it, and I don't want to risk you being bitten," she said. The thought of company had boosted her spirits for the first time since this whole ordeal started. But she'd made a commitment to Atlas, and he deserved follow-through. More than that, he deserved the world.

"We could bring in a trainer if it would make you feel better," he said. "And, for the record, I've been bitten before and lived to tell about it. The same will most likely happen again, so as long as he's had his rabies shot, we'll be good to go."

She chewed on the inside of her cheek, trying to think of a way to make it work. The idea of spending another night alone in her great-aunt's place wasn't the most appealing thought. It had served its purpose when she'd had no other option. Could she take Callum up on his offer?

"I'm not seeing how it would all work yet," she conceded. "Training takes time, and I don't want to stick Atlas outside in a barn. He would hate being left alone to fend for himself in a strange environment."

"How long has he been here and what else happened in Austin?" he asked.

"I picked him up the next day after the attack. A cop stood in my doorway as I packed a bag after they marked the place a crime scene. He told me they'd named my attacker's the Masked Monster. The last part was definitely true. Said that he might have been stalking me for a while before the attack since he knew my neighbor's name. I couldn't sleep in that place another night after what happened, so I left town," she admitted.

"Seems like Atlas has made himself right at home in a short time," he said. "How old is he?"

"A year and a half," she said.

"He's in a sweet spot for training," Callum noted. "Up until four years old, it's easier to train a dog. It can still be done after but requires a whole mess of patience and time."

"I've heard the saying about not being able to teach an old dog new tricks," she said.

"It's only half-true," he said. "If you don't think it's a good idea to leave here or you just don't want to, I'll understand. But it you *want* to stay across the

street and are struggling to work out the details…
don't. Just say yes and the rest can be figured out."

"I shouldn't," she said, thinking how much lonelier it was going to be here once he was gone. There was no good workaround for Atlas, and she wouldn't abandon him or treat him as an afterthought.

Callum stood up and walked over to the sink, cup in hand.

"At least take my number in case you change your mind or just need a hand with something," he said with his back to her.

The thought of him leaving caused her heart to pound wildly against the inside of her rib cage. Her pulse skyrocketed. The reaction she was having felt like more than fear. Fear she could handle. There wasn't a proper label for what she was experiencing. Or at least not one she could come up with at the moment.

Payton pulled it together with a couple of deep breaths and retrieved her cell phone. She handed it over while he stood at the kitchen sink.

"Thank you for offering a place to stay," she said as he took the cell from her hand. She couldn't help but wonder what the rough skin of his hands might feel like roaming all over her body. She coughed to clear a throat that had suddenly dried up faster than a well in a drought. "I appreciate it."

"If you change your mind, you'll know how to reach me," he said as he entered his contact information. Was his pulse pounding as much as hers?

"Believe it or not, just knowing there's someone

I can call if I get into trouble makes a huge difference," she said.

Callum handed over the phone when he was finished. Again, those rough hands briefly touched her skin, and more of that awareness skittered over her, electrifying her.

"We can figure out a plan for Atlas if he's holding you back from feeling comfortable saying yes," he continued. "We can even arrange for him to stay with you in the guest suite."

"It's tempting, but I think he'll be better off staying over here with me while I work on this place," she said. She rolled her shoulders a couple of times, trying to work out some of the tension that was returning. Her shoulder blades pinched together, causing pain to shoot down her back.

"Your call," he said before thanking her for the cup of coffee. "I'd better head back before my mother and grandmother send out a rescue squad."

His smile revealed perfectly straight, white teeth. But then, there was a whole lot more that was perfect about Callum Hayes. She appreciated his chivalry.

"I better get Atlas so you can leave," she said, thinking there was a lot she could do once he was gone to keep her mind off the event from seven days ago. A week. It had only been a week. It was only natural to feel unsettled so soon after the incident. She might not know the details of the bastard's face, but she would never forget his eyes. Or what it felt like to stare down the barrel of a handgun.

An involuntary shiver rocked her body as she

headed out to the porch first. She hooked Atlas's leash on and then walked him out to the backyard. Callum followed suit but stopped a few steps outside.

"Mind if I give your dog a treat?" he asked, shouting over Atlas's barks that were sounding off like a machine gun.

"Go ahead," she remarked, motioning toward the screened-in porch.

He turned and jogged inside as she forced her gaze away from the man's strong backside. Then he returned a few seconds later with a fistful of treats. Atlas's head, neck and ears were raised along with his hackles. His tail was stiff and his posture was like a bullet pointing toward Callum.

Callum, on the other hand, was the picture of relaxed. His arms were loose at his sides. His gaze moved slowly over the grass, not stopping for long on Atlas.

"Do you mind releasing him from his leash?" Callum asked.

"Is that smart?" she asked. "Won't he attack?"

"He could be coming at me right now. I suspect he felt cornered and caught off guard in the barn earlier. Out here, he has room to move and shouldn't feel so trapped." Callum's reasoning made sense, and she could only pray he was right. Then again, he was the one who'd been brought up on a ranch with animals everywhere.

Payton reached over and unclasped the leash, hovering just in case she needed to snap it back on.

"Good," Callum soothed before tossing a treat halfway in between them.

Atlas went for it, so Callum tossed two more, cutting down the distance just a little more. Atlas barked but went for the treats.

"That's enough for today," Callum said, holding his ground. "But he might be leash aggressive."

Payton moved beside her dog, surprised at the progress Callum had made in such a short time. "I'll keep that in mind. Thank you."

"You're welcome," Callum said before heading to his truck.

Her to-do list was piling up, and yet she stood there until his truck disappeared from view.

As she walked back to the barn, a noise beyond the tall grass to her left caught Atlas's attention. Teeth bared, a low growl tore from his throat. Fear gripped her.

## Chapter Four

Callum started up the engine of his truck with very little enthusiasm on his part. He wanted to blame his mood on not being ready to face the firing squad across the street. Between thinking about his past relationship and the news he needed to deliver to his mother and grandmother about not planning to leave his business, he wasn't quite ready to make the trek back.

Then there was Payton to consider. He hadn't lived in Cider Creek in a long time, but he believed it was safe. The fact she seemed like she needed to live off the grid angered him, too. No innocent person should be the one to hide. But since the bastard who'd targeted her had also most likely stalked her, according to the police, Callum understood her need to stay below the radar. He could only imagine the hell she'd been through during the ordeal.

He put the gearshift in Reverse and then turned the truck around. From somewhere deep within, he wanted her to feel safe here. As far as he could tell, she was doing an incredible job of handling the events leading up to her move. He wanted to do more than offer reassuring words.

Callum's heart ached for Payton, and he wished she'd taken him up on the offer to stay at the ranch. It was selfish. He could admit it. He wanted to be able to provide protection and make sure she was safe. No one would be stupid enough to attempt a break-in at the ranch.

The attraction he felt toward Payton and the chemistry between them was real. After what he'd been through, he no longer trusted his instincts when it came to the opposite sex. Those instincts were screaming at him now that Payton was different. *Unavailable* was probably a better word. Going on a date had to be the last thing on her mind after the—what had she said the law had called him?—the Masked Monster had set his sights on her. The question was whether or not he would allow her to get away with living when he'd wanted her dead.

Another burst of anger exploded in his chest at the thought. Since she wouldn't accept his offer to stay with her or take him up on the guest room at the ranch, there wasn't much he could do. Chewing on her situation wouldn't make a hill of beans' difference, no matter how much he wanted to help. Besides, he had a situation brewing back at home, and he needed to figure out how to tell his mother that he had no intention of leaving the company he'd built from the ground up to take over a ranch he had never asked for in the first place.

A wave of guilt stabbed him. Was he leaving his mother in a bad spot? How could he make her understand that he'd built and continued to run a business in Houston and, despite feeling a little lost lately, he had no intention of abandoning the employees who put their trust in him?

Could he explain his position straight out?

The other problem was that none of Callum's five siblings wanted to come back. They'd all moved on and built businesses in other places. No one was ready to jump ship and come home. How did he tell their mother no one wanted to live here? The thought of seeing the disappointment on her face after all she'd been through was a gut punch. Sometimes, being the oldest was more curse than blessing, since his younger siblings looked to him to step up in tough situations. They were all grown adults who were capable of standing up for themselves, don't get him wrong. It was decided their mother might be overwhelmed if they all showed up at once to tell her thanks, but no thanks to a life she'd worked her backside off alongside their grandfather to hand over someday.

With a heavy heart, he pulled into a parking spot in the small gravel lot beside the main house, where he would be staying. Facing down the front door twice in one day might not have been his brightest move, but he'd had to get out of there during the kitchen ambush. Despite Granny's good intentions, she'd been about to make the conversation a whole lot more awkward, which was saying something, considering Callum had been stumbling over his words.

His cell rang, breaking into the moment. He fished it out of his pocket and then checked the screen. Payton?

"Hello?" he answered. Instincts told him something wrong for her to be calling him this soon.

"Atlas," was all he heard through the static and wind. Payton sounded desperate. Had her dog run away?

"Payton," he said into the phone.

"Callum, please. Help. There's someone or something out there in the tall grass," she said before she let out a scream and the line went dead.

He couldn't have put the truck in Reverse any faster if he'd had a mechanical arm. His pulse kicked up a few notches. As the tires spit gravel, he caught sight of Granny in the kitchen window. The curtain was pulled back and she had a look of concern on her face. He waved, hoping the gesture would keep her from calling the sheriff.

Right now, he couldn't be concerned. Plus, now that he really thought about it, calling the sheriff wasn't such a bad idea. If Granny called, so be it. The lawman might be wasting his time, but he would be forgiving of an elderly woman. Callum, on the other hand, might get his behind chewed for the false alarm if that was what this turned out to be.

His mind also snapped to the possibility the intruder could be an animal and not her stalker. One of the cattle could have found a break in the fence and ended up on her property. It happened despite a rancher's best efforts. Paperwork and running fences to make sure the cattle stayed on property and in safe areas for them took up the lion's share of a rancher's day. Don't even get him started on calving season starting in February, sometimes earlier, when he'd learned to go weeks on end with only a few hours of sleep at night. The work had been brutal for a high schooler who was also an athlete. He and his siblings had spent summers trying to figure out how the heck they could move away in order to do their own things. Funny how prophetic their wishes had been.

Callum could admit to missing working side by side with his siblings. Everyone was so busy now they rarely, if ever, saw one another. There had been something special about working those long hours and bonding over sweat equity in the ranch.

Their grandfather had been hard on each one of them, and probably Callum most of all. Being the oldest got him chewed out the most when any of his siblings made a mistake or flat out did something they shouldn't have.

Not more than a couple minutes had passed by the time Callum was pulling up next to the Baker farmhouse. He scanned the area for Payton, his heart pounding harder with every second he couldn't find her. He surveyed the grassy area closest to the barn. It had to be the spot she'd referred to…and nothing.

And then he heard a bloodcurdling scream that had him jumping out of his truck and racing toward the back side of the barn. Atlas's yelp nearly cracked Callum's chest in two pieces.

As Callum rounded the barn, he caught a glimpse of Payton as she was bolting toward the sound of the yelp.

"Atlas," she shouted, and the desperation in her voice was a punch to the solar plexus.

Rather than try to shout over her, Callum made a beeline toward her. He admired her for the way she ran toward Atlas without knowing what she was up against. Her love for the animal tugged at Callum's heartstrings. There was a good dog inside Atlas, just waiting for the right person with the right patience to coax it out of him. Callum had never been more certain of anything in his life, and he wanted to help. Those two needed each other more than he'd realized. He was beginning to understand why Payton would volunteer to sleep in the dilapidated farmhouse on a temporary mattress rather than a comfy bed in the guest room across the street. His respect for her grew by the minute.

And so did his feelings.

Atlas cried out again. Either someone had him and was torturing him, or he'd been caught by a wild boar or coyote. Knowing which would be nice. Callum could surprise a human and catch him off guard if that was the case. He would need to be stealth. But with an animal? Callum needed to help Payton make the most noise possible to scare it off. He couldn't let himself go there—wondering if Atlas was mortally wounded. Instead, he pushed his legs as fast as they would go to catch up to Payton. She and Atlas both would fare a lot better with him in the picture. Another animal would bolt in one case. In the other— well, at least Payton wouldn't be facing the bastard alone.

"ATLAS, BABY." Payton heard heavy footsteps behind her as she saw a glimpse of her sweet dog struggling to get up. Whatever had been there a few seconds ago was gone now, and she hadn't gotten a glimpse to know if it was a man or an animal. She bit back a curse as she dropped down to her knees. Hot tears streaked her cheeks, blurring her vision.

"How and where is he hurt?" Callum's deep baritone rolled over her and through her, calming her nerves to a notch below panic.

Atlas's thick fur wasn't showing any visible signs of blood as she searched for his injury. He was panting hard, and the way he looked at her with those soulful eyes threatened to suck her under.

"What do I do?" she asked, wishing she had more experience with animals so she could stop Atlas's suffering.

"Move to his head and try to keep his gaze on you so I can check him out," Callum said.

She immediately repositioned, stroking the dog's head and neck as Callum smoothed his hand over Atlas's torso. He yelped when Callum's hand moved to his underside. When Callum pulled his hand back, bright red blood soaked his fingers.

Callum muttered a string of curses under his breath. They were the exact ones Payton was thinking.

"We need to get him inside. I can call the local vet and have someone out here in less than half an hour. In the meantime, I'll do what I can to figure out the damage," he said. "I'll pick him up if you'll distract him."

"Callum, I can't let you do that. His bite will be ten times worse while he's scared," she warned.

"That may be, but I'm not about to leave him out here, and if the stalker is the one responsible for this, that means we're sitting ducks right now," he stated, and he was right.

Payton glanced around, searching for those horrible blue eyes that had haunted her dreams for a solid week. She issued a sharp sigh. There was no choice to make when she really thought about it. Callum was a grown man who was well aware of the risks he was proposing. Plus, he was right. They needed to get out of here and into the barn at the very least.

"How about the barn?" she asked, thinking it was much closer.

"That'll work, too," he responded, leaning forward and scooping the hundred-pound dog into his arms like Atlas weighed nothing. She noted that Callum had positioned himself behind the dog in a position that made it nearly impossible for Atlas to reach around and bite.

"Good, boy," she said to her dog, trying to keep his attention on her as she stroked a hand over the back of his neck.

Callum wasted no time breaking into a run. The fact they were potentially in serious danger nailed her as they neared the barn. She broke ahead to open the door in time for Callum to bolt through it. He glanced around, no doubt looking for a good place to set Atlas down.

"I'll grab the horse's blanket," she said, running to a stall before pulling the blanket off the door. Callum was only a couple of steps behind her, and she reasoned he would want Atlas to be able to see her at all times. Atlas seemed resigned to being carried, but she feared he would spasm at any moment and force himself to be dropped so he could get down. She needed to move fast so that wouldn't happen.

"Right here is fine," Callum said.

Payton folded the blanket and placed it near his boots. He immediately set down Atlas, who surprisingly didn't fight back. He did, however, try to snap his neck back a couple of times like he was trying to bite.

"You're okay," she soothed, managing as calm a voice as she could muster while her pulse pounded and she tried to catch her breath. She dropped down beside Atlas as he curled up and tried to lick his hindquarters.

"He's been bitten," Callum said as he wiped blood on his jeans and then fished his cell phone out of his front pocket. "I'm guessing he is up-to-date on his rabies shots, since you got him from the shelter."

"He is," she reassured.

"Doesn't protect him from feral swine disease,

but I'll take what we can get," he said as he made a call. He turned around and took a couple of steps in the opposite direction as he made the call, but Payton's mind ran rampant. Living in Texas her whole life, she'd heard stories of feral hogs. This was her first dog, and she was clearly in way over her head living out here. A familiar helpless feeling tried to grab hold, but she refused to let it take root. Not again. There was some relief in knowing an animal was responsible instead of the person she feared most. She held on to it.

"You're going to be okay, Atlas," she said through blurry eyes and tearstained cheeks. "I promise I'll do everything I can to help."

Atlas was panting hard. She glanced around for his water bowl in case he was thirsty, found it. By the time she retrieved it and set it next to Atlas's snout, Callum had ended his call.

"Vet is on his way," he said. "He's coming as fast as he can."

"What can we do in the meantime?" she asked, urging Atlas to drink.

"Keep him as comfortable as possible," he said. "Do you have any hand sanitizer out here?"

"As a matter of fact, it's right here." She retrieved the pump bottle and closed the distance between them.

"Until we know exactly what we're dealing with, we'll have to take precautions," he stated, cupping his hands and extending them toward her. She squirted the gel-like liquid into his palms before doing the same to her own. "Do you have any gloves?"

"Inside the house," she said, immediately turning toward the farmhouse. "I'll just—"

"Stay with Atlas," he said. "I'll grab them if you tell me where they are."

She realized the underlying meaning of what he was saying. It was safer for her to stay here in the barn with Atlas rather than be exposed by running out in the open toward the farmhouse.

"Under the kitchen sink," she said on a sharp sigh. Then added, "Be careful."

Callum shot a smile that almost looked casual.

"I'll be right back," he said. "Promise."

She prayed he could keep that commitment, because a growing part of her wanted to lean into his strength.

# Chapter Five

Callum sprinted toward the farmhouse, hoping like hell he wasn't about to have to try to dodge a bullet along the way. All signs pointed to an animal being responsible for Atlas's injuries, but he would take nothing for granted.

The Masked Monster had a personal stake in seeing to it Payton couldn't identify him or testify in court. This was also personal, considering he seemed to handpick his victims. Although *victim* didn't seem like the right word for Payton. *Target* seemed a better choice.

The box of rubber cleaning gloves was right where Payton said they would be. He grabbed them along with the roll of paper towels sitting on the counter. He glanced around to see if there was anything else he could use and grabbed an empty cleaning bucket by the handle and filled it with water. There were no suds, so that was a good sign there weren't any remnants of soap inside. He could use the supplies to clean up as much of the injury as possible to see what the vet would really be dealing with after he arrived.

In the meantime, Callum wasn't one to sit on his hands and do nothing. He kept one ear trained on the barn as he gathered up the supplies and then headed back toward Payton. Water sloshed around, and he figured that he probably lost half the bucket's contents by the time he made it to the barn.

Payton was on her knees, bent over Atlas's head as he lay there panting.

"I can't get him to drink anything, but he seems thirsty," she said. The tenderness in her voice when she spoke about her dog warmed his heart.

"He's not panting because he's thirsty," Callum said as he joined her. "It's also how a dog shows he's in pain."

"What else can we do?" she asked, alternating between wringing her hands together and gently comforting Atlas.

"Make him comfortable until Raul arrives," he stated. "I'll clean up as much as I can, but I don't want to stress him out more than he already is."

Atlas lay on his side, the whites of his eyes visible as he panted heavily. At least he wasn't trying to get up and run away, and he'd shifted to lying on his good side.

"Let's see what's happening back here." Slowly and carefully, Callum knelt down with the supplies. Sudden movements would only startle Atlas, and his defenses were already on high alert. The dog kept one eye on Callum at all times and popped his snout around more than once for an attempt at a bite as he cleaned the area the best he could. "Looks like he was gored." A quick glance at Payton said she had no idea what that meant. "Wild hogs have tusks and aren't afraid to use them."

"He'll be all right. Won't he?" The sound of panic in her voice was a gut punch.

"Raul—Dr. Sanchez—is the best vet in the county, probably the state," Callum reassured her, wishing there was something he could say to ease her concerns. The truth was that he couldn't make any promises. At least none he could guarantee that he could keep. And after being cheated on and lied to by his ex, he would never make anyone else feel as awful as he had. Five years of his life and his hopes for a future had gone down the drain in a matter of minutes when he'd opened an office door. That was all it had taken to obliterate his life. So, no, he wouldn't lie.

For now, he would just stem the bleeding as they waited for Raul.

The family's go-to vet lived down the street. It didn't take long for him to come roaring up. Payton volunteered to wave him down. She pushed to standing and took off before Callum could remind her that leaving him alone with Atlas might not be the best move.

For the moment, Atlas seemed to realize Callum was there to help. That, or he was too weak to put up much of a fight. The latter worried Callum the most.

"You're going to be just fine," he reassured Atlas in as calm a tone as he could manage. His brothers had teased him about being an animal whisperer when they were young. They'd said the cattle always calmed down whenever Callum showed up. It used to embarrass him, but now he hoped a little bit of it was true. He could use all the help he could get with Atlas. His heart went out to the animal, who was only trying to protect Payton. "And don't worry. I'll look after her while you recover. You and me are a team now."

He meant it, too. There was no way he was leaving Payton to her own defenses with a dog who needed tending to. He hadn't exactly figured out how he intended to convince her to let him stay. The words hadn't come to him yet. And, clearly, it was always her choice. All he could hope was to come up with an argument convincing enough to have her reconsider his earlier offer of help.

There was no way he would get any sleep knowing she was across the street and vulnerable. This time, it had been a wild hog. What about next time? What if the Monster tracked her down and showed up?

Payton needed backup.

Speaking of Payton, she came rushing in with Raul next to her.

"Looks like he's been gored," Callum immediately said to Raul as the vet rushed over, black bag in hand. "It's pretty serious."

Callum didn't make eye contact with Payton after his comment, because his heart would break in half at her expression. He hadn't sugarcoated the situation a few minutes ago. Still, she probably hadn't been expecting him to speak so bluntly, but Raul needed to know the severity of what he was dealing with.

Raul came around to Callum's side as Payton returned to her spot. The vet reached into his bag and pulled out gloves as Payton spoke in a whisper and stroked Atlas's neck. Her presence calmed the dog considerably. The two might have only been together for a short time, but their connection made it seem like a lot longer.

After an inspection, Raul looked up at Payton.

"I'm going to give him a shot to calm him and help him relax so I can assess what we're dealing with here," Raul said. "Keep doing what you're doing. He'll feel a pinch when I insert the needle, but that's all, and it'll only last a couple of seconds. Okay?"

One of Raul's many good traits was how willing he was to spend the extra couple of seconds to explain what was happening and what he was about to do. Folks responded well to his bedside manner. His calming presence around animals didn't hurt, either.

"Yes, okay," she said as she refocused her energy on Atlas.

Callum stayed put so as not to agitate Atlas. He would be calmer if he knew where everyone was. Sudden movements might cause him to snap, and no one wanted him to be any more uncomfortable than he already had to be.

Raul worked in his opened bag that was sitting beside him, most likely preparing the needle.

"I'm going to do this quickly, so as long as everyone is ready," Raul said before searching Payton's eyes and then Callum's.

Both of them nodded at exactly the same time.

Raul administered the shot, Atlas yelped and Payton reassured the animal. He didn't try to bite this time, and Callum saw that as progress. He might not be an animal whisperer, but this guy had been through a lot in one day, and the last thing Callum wanted to do was add to Atlas's pain. Granny truly had the magic touch with animals. If there'd been time and he'd been thinking straight, he would have called on her in the first place.

Granny didn't drive and had come to live with her daughter on the ranch not long after Callum had been born, but he never counted her out for finding a way around things. The woman could pull out a miracle when she needed to. There'd been plenty of times in his childhood when she'd surprised him and figured a way around Duncan's decree that none of his grandkids should do anything besides work the ranch. When his grandfather had nixed the idea of Callum playing on the basketball team even if, as promised, he kept up his chores during calving season, Granny had enlisted the coach's help. He'd offered extra credit to anyone who helped Callum out, and, suddenly, the whole team was showing up before school so Callum could stay after for practice.

Duncan hadn't made a secret out of not being amused. Callum's mother had spent plenty of hours smoothing things over while her own mother stood in the kitchen every morning handing out coffee to Callum's teammates.

Callum smiled at the memory. He'd forgotten so many of the good times about living here, allowing the fights with his grandfather to overshadow them.

The realization struck hard. Guilt quickly followed. His grandfather was gone, and Callum didn't want to hold on to the bad memories any longer. It was time to let them go, despite the fact that he'd never gotten closure. He'd never gotten to sit down with the man and have a friendly conversation over a fishing pole while holding a beer. Shame, he thought.

Now he would never get the chance to make things right between them.

PAYTON WATCHED AS the tension in Atlas's body relaxed. She would be forever grateful to Callum and his family's vet. At five feet nine inches, give or take, Raul Sanchez had jet-black hair, olive-colored skin and kind brown eyes. Next to Callum, the man would be considered small, but in truth he was about average for the men she'd known in Austin. She involuntarily shivered at the thought that he was very close to the size and build of her attacker.

Would she measure every man she met that way from this day forward? Around the Masked Monster's size? Smaller? Larger? Would she search everyone's eyes, looking for his?

She hated the thought that the horrific event would define her life from now on. Instead of giving in, she vowed to find a way past it or through it. Granted, that would be impossible to do while he was still out there, lurking around, preying on others and/or stalking her. The only way she could put this behind her and get closure was if he was brought to justice. Getting him off the streets would go a long way toward giving her the confidence she needed to push past what he'd done.

Right now, at least, Atlas was getting the care he needed. Head down, gaze intent, Raul was focused on stitching up the wound. He'd given Atlas another shot to numb the area. He'd shaved his side. And then he'd worked quickly and diligently while Atlas drifted off into a comfortable sleep. He had to be exhausted from the fight.

"Atlas is very brave," Callum said, his voice barely above a whisper. "He most likely gave chase, and the hog felt backed into a corner."

"I read the book *Old Yeller* when I was a kid. That's the extent of my knowledge," she said, unable to even think about the possibility anything like that could happen to Atlas.

"Raul would do everything possible to ensure Atlas didn't suffer the same fate, but since he's vaccinated against rabies that won't be a concern here," Callum said. "Hogs are violent creatures. In this case, injuries are a bigger threat."

"I had no idea they were even in the area," she said. "I guess coming here unprepared wasn't my brightest idea."

"You did what you had to in order to survive," he quickly countered. "You adopted a dog that literally hates men and came to a place where you couldn't be easily tracked. I'd say you're doing all right so far."

She reached over and touched his hand. An unexpected jolt of electricity rocketed through her at the point of contact. She stared at her fingers for a long moment, confused by the reaction. It couldn't have been static electricity. Not unless it had been amped up by a hundred notches. Besides, this didn't hurt. In fact, it felt pretty amazing, sending aftershocks of warmth vibrating through her.

All it took was one look at Atlas to kill the vibe.

"He looks so helpless lying there," she said to Callum. "The only thing keeping me sane at this point is the fact I know he's in good hands."

A thought struck. How on earth was she going to afford this? A home visit from a vet wasn't going to come cheap, and she was struggling as it was without her barista job. Spending all that money on tuition suddenly seemed like a bad idea. At this point, she should cut her losses and drop out. Plenty of people made successes out of themselves without an advanced degree. She could do the same. Besides, with the Masked Monster parading around, she was the one locked away, hiding.

A new sense of resolve kicked in at just how unfair it would be for her to stop living her life while the bastard stalked his next victim. With no way to identify him, she was at a loss as to how to help find him and ensure he was locked behind bars. There were no other victims who were still alive. There had been no DNA evidence found at her apartment that was useful to the case so far, but then, they'd said processing took time. Austin PD had half admitted they were trying to figure out the killer's pattern while waiting for him to strike again.

They'd put up posters on campus, warning students to be on the lookout for his general description. The only thing they had going for them at this point was his MO.

The guy was intelligent, or he would have been caught by now. He was resourceful, that was certain, and he seemed to know a lot about disarming women. Rapists and murderers who weren't smart ended up locked behind bars before they had a chance to make their crimes a habit.

"He's doing great," Raul reassured, never breaking concentration from the task at hand. "He's a real trouper."

Payton twisted her fingers together for lack of something better to do. In a short time, Atlas had wormed his way into her heart, and she couldn't imagine being here without him. He'd allowed her to get at least a little bit of sleep the first night here, and things had improved since then. Despite promising herself she wouldn't let him sleep on her makeshift bed, she'd failed miserably. He slept curled up at her feet and was a surprisingly good foot warmer.

After welcoming him into her heart, she didn't have it in her to make him sleep on the floor. Besides, he wasn't exactly coming home to a mansion with the farmhouse. The place would be nice eventually, if Payton didn't run out of funds before making it livable.

Again, she thought about a hefty vet bill and started working her fingers.

Callum placed a calming hand over hers, and more of that warmth traveled over her and through her.

"Everything okay?" he asked before adding, "Aside from the obvious?"

"I can't use a credit card, for obvious reasons, and it's dawning on me that I'm not sure if I can afford Raul even if I could," she whispered. "Of course, I want Atlas to have the best care, and—"

"He's on retainer for my family," Callum said. "There won't be a bill."

"What does that even mean?" she asked, a little more than stunned.

"Just that he doesn't itemize. We pay a monthly stipend, and he takes care of all our needs," Callum explained. "So, there's no need to worry about a bill."

Payton couldn't even begin to fathom what that was like. She was beginning to see that she wasn't dealing with an ordinary family when it came to the Hayes bunch. Their home wasn't visible from the street, so she had no idea what it looked like, and she hadn't really considered that her great-aunt might live across the street from the kind of wealth that had the best vet in the state on retainer. Although her great-aunt had mentioned the fact that her neighbors weren't hurting for much.

"There," Raul said. "That should do it." He sat back on his heels, practically beaming with pride. "I'll give you pain medication to keep him comfortable for the next couple of days. It might also stop him from messing with the stitches, but he'll have to wear a cone, too, and my guess is that he's not going to like it."

"How is he, though? Really? Is he out of the woods?" Payton asked, her heart pounding in her throat.

"Unfortunately, I won't know the answer for a couple of weeks. Right now, I'm not seeing anything of concern, but it can take time to know if he's been infected," Raul said. He ran down a list of symptoms to watch for that would require an immediate call. He threw out terms like *brucellosis* and *leptospirosis as he reassured her the dose of antibiotics should be effective against both*. Her brain couldn't fathom any of those diseases taking Atlas's life while he was so young. Guilt for letting him get loose nailed her.

"I know that sounds like a lot," Raul finally said after she'd zoned out. "But, right now, he's doing great, and our main concern is keeping him from ripping out those stitches."

"Thank you," she said. "For everything. Now I know what to watch out for, and I'll keep my eyes on him 24/7."

Raul smiled as he pulled each glove off, placed them in a baggie and then cleaned up the area. He set down a bottle of pills before detailing out the schedule. "These should help with any pain."

"He'll be comfortable, Raul," Callum said. "We'll make sure of it."

Payton caught the word *we'll*. Did she dare hope she wasn't alone in this? Hope could be a dangerous thing. Hope had her thinking she could fix up her great-aunt's place, finish the semester and slide right past a serial killer undetected.

Could hope allow her to open her heart to Callum even just a little?

## Chapter Six

Callum walked Raul to his truck. On the way out of the barn, he surveyed the area for any signs of threat. Payton was still shaken up by Atlas's hog encounter, but this whole situation could have ended a whole lot worse.

"Thank you for coming by on such short notice," Callum said to Raul. As much as Cider Creek had changed since Callum had left all those years ago, it was comforting to know some things stayed the same. Raul's father had been the family vet before Raul had taken the reins of the family business.

"I have to admit, I was surprised to hear your voice," Raul said as he tucked his bag in the back seat of his dual cab pickup. "When did you get back to town?"

"This morning." Callum chuckled. He couldn't help himself. Word traveled fast, and it would be all over town that he was home by this time tomorrow. The gossip mill wasn't his favorite part of small-town living. It also occurred to him news would spread about him being with Payton, which was the last thing she needed. He was sure tongues were already wagging since she was so secretive. Being attached to a Hayes would most definitely not help her fly under the radar.

"Welcome home," Raul said before catching Callum's gaze and holding it. They'd been in the same grade in school and had played on a couple of sports teams together. "You are staying now that your grandfather is gone, right?"

"Nothing has been decided," he said, not really wanting to play his hand right here even though he hoped he could trust Raul.

"Well, it's good to see you either way." Raul extended a hand, which Callum took. The two engaged in a vigorous handshake, and it reminded Callum of old times.

"Good to see you, man," he said with a smile. He wasn't exactly sure how to be delicate with the current situation, but the notion word was about to spread about the beautiful young woman in the farmhouse meant he had to say something. Since the right words escaped him, he just went with the first ones that came to him, "I'd appreciate discretion about Payton and her dog."

"I'm not one for gossip," Raul said. "So, I'll do my best not to be offended by that comment. However, I do have a wife who will pump me for answers when I get home, and since she has my phone on one of those tracking apps in case I get tied up and can't respond right away, I'll have to tell her something."

Callum nodded. He could appreciate his friend's

predicament and, heaven knew, he had no business getting between a husband and his wife. Protecting Payton was still his top priority, so he needed to figure out a way to do both without putting Raul in a bad position.

"I appreciate your confidence, Raul," Callum said. "And I have no right to ask you not to be honest with Alice. She's your wife, and that's a sacred bond."

"Yes," Raul agreed. "I thought you were with someone." He glanced at Callum's ring finger.

"Didn't work out," he said.

"Sorry to hear it." Raul seemed genuinely upset that he'd asked.

"Don't be," he said, waving him off. Going into the details held no appeal. "Sometimes these things fizzle out."

"I'm still sorry," Raul said.

"And I appreciate it," Callum countered. He did. He appreciated Raul's sincerity, and he appreciated the fact he could trust his old sports buddy. "Is there any way to limit the details about what happened here without being dishonest with Alice?"

Raul stood there, studying Callum for a long moment.

"This is really important to you, isn't it?" Raul finally asked.

"For now, it is," he said. "In a few days when the reason Payton is here gets sorted out, that might be a different story."

"I can keep the questions at bay until then without breaking any marriage vows," Raul said. "Besides,

GPS isn't one hundred percent accurate all the time. It might seem like I'm across the street or had to come here because something got loose. I don't have to mention the fact you're back or that I met the mystery guest who is currently living here."

"As long as it won't get you into any trouble," Callum stated with a sigh of relief. "I would owe you one."

"After being married for almost a decade, my wife doesn't exactly stare at the phone all night. She knows I'm on call and isn't surprised when I have to take off," he said. "Besides, I think it's margarita night with her and Ellie Reynolds. Remember her?"

"How could I forget? We dated all of freshman year," Callum said.

"She's still single," Raul said with a smile and a wink. "Technically divorced, but that's the same thing, right?"

"Since when did you become the town's matchmaker?" Callum quipped, appreciating the easygoing conversation. It was almost like the last twenty years disappeared and he and Raul could pick right back up where they left off.

"Now I'm hurt," Raul said, clutching his chest. He fished his keys out of his pocket. "On a serious note, make sure Atlas keeps the cone on. I know it looks uncomfortable and it's going to drive him up the wall. But it's important."

Callum was already nodding.

"You know I'm one hundred percent in when it

comes to this animal's recovery. I'll do whatever it takes to get him back to good health," Callum said.

"Sounds like you are sticking around after all," Raul said with a pat on Callum's back. "Keep me posted on his progress. You're from around here—you know what signs to watch for."

"I do and I will," Callum said. Of course, it was up to Payton. But if she gave him the green light, he would see this through to at least get her and Atlas over the hump.

"Keep in touch," Raul said as he climbed into his truck. "And I hope to see you around."

"I'm here for a little while," Callum said. "No promises on how long that'll be, but I'd like to see you and Alice before I take off."

"Sounds good," Raul said before closing the door. He backed out of the drive and was on his way a moment later.

Callum stood there and waved like he somehow belonged here. As though this were his home and he was seeing off a guest. He shook his head before turning around toward the barn. Keeping the grassy area in his peripheral, he couldn't help but think local wildlife wasn't Payton's biggest threat while living alone out here. Now that Atlas was hurt, she was even more vulnerable.

Walking into the barn, seeing her cradling Atlas's head while he was in la-la land from the pain medication, nearly broke Callum's heart. He cleared his throat so as not to startle her.

"I'm so grateful for everything you've done for

us," Payton started before he had a chance to open his mouth. "I don't have any friends in town and didn't know who else to call."

"You did the right thing," he reassured. "I'd be upset if you didn't reach out and I heard about this in some other way."

"But I don't know how to repay your kindness," she continued without looking up. "I'm thankful, and I'll figure out a way to—"

"Kindness is a gift that doesn't need repaying," he said. "Then it would be called something else entirely, like a trade or a business exchange. In this case, when you're in a position to do something for someone else…do it. That's all the repayment I need."

"It's just so much with Atlas's injury," she continued. When she looked up, tears streaked her cheeks, and his chest squeezed.

"During calving season, this potentially would have been a bigger sacrifice. Now, Raul is on retainer and probably wanted something to do with his time," Callum countered.

Speaking of Raul, how strange was it that someone he went to high school with and played on the same sports teams with had already been married for a decade? Raul had children. All of Callum's cousins were now married. Callum had been on the same road to matrimony. Since his ex-fiancée ended up sleeping with someone else, he was grateful it had happened before they'd walked down the aisle. Marriage wasn't a commitment he took lightly, and he wouldn't have been able to walk away once he'd made a vow. Looking at the situation in that light made it seem like she did him a favor. After spending months nursing a broken heart, he would disagree. Still, it was so much better than finding out she was in love with someone else a month into the marriage. The whole experience had put a bad taste in his mouth when it came to making a commitment. It only seemed like a matter of time before the day in and day out nuts and bolts of a relationship would wear thin. If he was being totally honest, he could admit the sizzle had been gone for a long time from his relationship with Hannah. He'd loved her out of habit more than anything else. Wasn't that what all relationships eventually became?

His mother and father had managed to fall into a marital rhythm. He'd been a good man who loved his wife and kids.

"If the offer is still open, I'd like to sleep in your guest room tonight," Payton said, shocking him out of his reverie.

"Absolutely," he said, allowing himself a small smile.

"Are you sure it's no trouble?" Payton asked.

"Are you kidding me?" he asked. "You'll be doing me a favor by distracting my mother, who, by the way, will be thrilled when I call her to let her know you'll be staying with us. The downstairs guest suite will be good for you and Atlas. It's close to the front door, and you'll be able to leash Atlas to go outside."

"Sounds perfect," she said. "I can't imagine sleeping in the farmhouse while he's in this condition."

Callum didn't want to admit just how relieved he

was at hearing this news. He didn't want to need to know that Payton and Atlas were going to be fine. Someone should clue his heart in, because it seemed to have a mind of its own when it came to the beautiful woman and her dog.

"SINCE HE'S OUT, I'll have no problem picking him up and getting him settled into the truck," Callum offered. "It'll give you time to run inside and pack a bag."

"I won't take long," Payton said, figuring she only needed enough to get through the night. She could always come back tomorrow if she decided to stay longer. Her nerves were shot after the events of the day, and she'd worked herself into a lather worrying about what might happen next.

"Take all the time you need," Callum said as he walked around to the other side of her sweet sleeping boy. "We'll be in the truck."

Callum fished out his key fob before unlocking the truck.

"Can you manage all right?" she asked as she gently laid Atlas's head down. As she stood up, she realized she had blood on her clothes. She would have to change into something clean. She didn't want to scare Callum's mother or grandmother by showing up looking like she'd been in a fight and lost.

"I've got this," he said, and it sure was nice for someone to have her back for a change. The concept was foreign to her, but she could get used to it. Should she allow herself to, though?

Right now, she would take all the help she could get as she thanked Callum and then headed toward the house. She hesitated on the back porch, wondering if someone had slipped inside like in those horror movies.

Payton shook it off. She was psyching herself out for no reason. Besides, Callum had been in here a little while ago grabbing those gloves and the paper towels he used to clean up Atlas's injury. Speaking of Atlas, she would keep close watch on him for the next couple of weeks to make sure he didn't develop anything life-threatening. As bad as being gored was, he could recover from it and completely heal with time.

Working over here was going to be difficult while he was recovering. It was impossible not to feel like life was stacked against her and everything that could go wrong was. A little voice in the back of her mind picked that moment to point out that a modern-day knight in shining armor had shown up this morning, with muffins, no less. To say the day had been a mixed blessing sounded about right.

Payton steeled her resolve and headed inside the farmhouse. She didn't waste time washing her hands, peeling off her clothes and then throwing on a clean pair of jeans and a blouse. She didn't have anything fancy, but meeting Callum's mother and grandmother in a jogging suit didn't seem polite. Instead, the jogging suit went into her overnight bag, along with toiletries. After packing her toothbrush, she got a glimpse of herself in the mirror. All she could think was *what a mess*.

Taking a few extra minutes to throw on concealer and brighten her lips with a tinted gloss wouldn't throw them off schedule. Besides, what schedule? Callum didn't seem in a hurry to rush across the street. Aside from her stomach reminding her she needed nourishment soon, she wasn't eager to meet new folks, either. She'd already met two people today—people who could talk to others. She wasn't worried about Callum. He was fully aware of what had brought her to Cider Creek and knew the stakes when it came to keeping her identity a secret. As it was, she'd had to buy gift cards with cash to have necessary items delivered. She was going to great lengths not to draw attention to herself while renovating the farmhouse. As long as her name didn't get out, she would be okay.

Payton placed her overnight bag by the back door in the kitchen. The dry dog food was in the pantry, half-full, which would make carrying the fifty-pound bag more manageable. She could do this in two trips. She picked up Atlas's food and brought that out first. Callum met her halfway and took the bag from her. He loaded it in the bed of the pickup.

Her overnight bag was an easy grab. She locked the door behind her and turned toward Callum, who stood there leaning a slender hip on his truck. Her heart performed a little flip at the sight of him, and her stomach fluttered as though a dozen butterflies had suddenly been released.

Pushing those emotions aside, she gripped the handle of her bag a little tighter and crossed the yard to his vehicle, wondering what in tarnation she'd just gotten herself into.

## Chapter Seven

Callum parked in the same spot he had earlier. He was beginning to notice how long it had been since breakfast, and he wanted to get Payton and Atlas settled and comfortable before dinner. He wasn't kidding earlier; his mother would be thrilled to have company, and she was more than curious about the new neighbor. Marla Hayes would die before she would be viewed as a nosy neighbor. This would give his mother a chance to see that Payton was a good and decent person. The annoying voice in the back of his mind wanted to add a couple more adjectives to her description, like *smart*, *compassionate* and *sinning-on-Sunday beautiful*.

He ignored it.

Besides, once his mother and grandmother met Payton, they would want to take her under their wings. She couldn't ask for better or more caring neighbors. Nosy? Well, he wouldn't lie. They were. They also knew how to keep a secret and would keep an eye out for Payton. Since he didn't plan on sticking around forever, he would feel a whole lot better if Payton had his family looking out for her once he was gone. They wouldn't be able to help but fall in love with her once they got to know her.

Plus, there was Atlas to consider. It would be good for him to be around other folks besides Payton. He needed to acclimate to the area and get to know the people he would run into from time to time so she felt comfortable taking him into town with her.

"I'll grab him if you can get your overnight bag," he said to Payton as he shut off the engine.

She nodded, and he noticed she'd been quiet on the way over.

"You're not having second thoughts, are you?" he asked.

"No," she said. "At least, I don't think so. I am nervous about meeting your mother and grandmother. What if they don't like me? Or want Atlas in the house? He is a handful."

"They'll love you," he quickly countered, trying to shut down that line of thinking before it could seed.

"*Love* might be a strong word," she said. "I'll take not offended by."

"Believe me, you have nothing to worry about with those two," he said with a smile. "They're good people, and they like helping others. I'm surprised your great-aunt didn't introduce you already."

"I wasn't allowed to visit often," she explained. "When I did, I think she wanted to keep me all to herself, since I was in and out so fast."

"Ranchers get very little time off, so I'm sure that didn't help," he said.

"Do you think it's too much to ask them to keep my situation a secret for a while?" she asked.

"I'll ask, but I have no doubt they'll respect your privacy," he said. "They're curious about you. There isn't a whole lot of movement in Cider Creek. The whole town is probably wondering who you are and why you decided to move here."

"That's what I'm afraid of," she said on a sharp sigh before reaching for her overnight bag. She exited the vehicle before he had a chance to soothe her worries. But then, the proof was in the pudding. All Payton had to do was meet his mother and granny to realize her fears weren't justified. They were, however, understandable after what she'd been through, and he didn't blame her one bit for having them.

"People will put two and two together and figure that you're related to Ms. Baker." He scooped up Atlas and kicked the door shut behind him. He could lock up later.

She nodded.

"Besides, Raul's wife will get all kinds of tongues wagging about my presence back in town," he said. The gossip mill wasn't something he was looking forward to while he was home.

"Wow, by the way," Payton said, freezing as she took a step toward the main house.

"It's impressive," he said. "Feels less...*grand* once you get inside."

"This is a house?" she asked. "I had no idea something this big sat across the street from my aunt's much smaller place. It's strange."

"My grandfather liked his privacy, too, which is why none of the house is visible from the street," Callum said. The man had been far too private for Callum's taste. He'd never gotten close to his grandkids as a result, always keeping Callum and his siblings at arm's length. *Stubborn* was another word that came to mind when thinking about his grandfather. The combination didn't exactly make for a warm and fuzzy male parental figure. But their mother more than made up for it, and Granny was a character and she was clear with her affection for her grandchildren.

He walked up to the front door.

"Do you mind?" he asked, motioning toward the knob, but Payton was already on it, sidestepping him and reaching for the handle. She opened the door and moved over so he could walk in first. He did, then took the first right down the long hallway leading toward her quarters. The guest suite took up the last two doors and was always ready despite his mother not having company in the past year following her father-in-law's death.

"This could be an apartment," she said, setting her bag down by the door and twisting her hands together. "In fact, it's bigger than anyplace I've ever lived. My great-aunt's place will be the largest home I've ever lived in, and it would fit in a fraction of this entire house."

Callum had forgotten how impressive the main house was to others. Growing up here, he never gave it much thought. But having plenty of space didn't equal being treated like little princes. Hard work and discipline came hand-in-hand with ranching life. They had a way of keeping a person grounded.

"The set of French doors leads out to a patio area. It'll be a good place for Atlas to relieve himself," he explained as he looked around for a spot for Atlas. If he set the dog on the bed, he might roll off and get hurt. The flooring was carpet, but he could land funny and hurt himself all over again. With the medications, Callum didn't want to risk it.

"He always sleeps with me," Payton said, seeming to catch on to what was going on. "But I'm guessing that's not safe."

"Probably not a good idea, since he's doped up," Callum agreed. "I can put him down on the bed for now until we figure out a better solution."

He did, and Payton sat down beside her dog. She was loyal and compassionate. Atlas had found a good home with her. He'd done good.

Callum searched around.

"I can pile up a bunch of blankets on the floor near the bed so you can keep an eye on him," he said.

"Or would it be too much trouble to put the mattress directly on the floor?" she asked. "That way, it wouldn't matter if he rolled off. He wouldn't have far to go. Plus, I won't sleep a wink if he'd not next to me."

The dog didn't just do good. He hit the jackpot.

"I'll just move—"

"We could move it off together," she cut him off. "That way he won't be disturbed."

"We can do that," he said, impressed with her dedication and willingness to roll her sleeves up. Hannah had been the opposite. She would have worried too much about breaking her nails—nails that she had to maintain with weekly appointments. "I'll take this side."

Comparisons were hard, though. Hannah hadn't been so into appearances in the beginning of their relationship. In fact, she'd started fussing over her nails and her appearance about the same time Trey had come on board. Looking back, Callum should have seen the signs. Hannah had wanted to welcome Trey by having him over for cookouts on Sundays. She'd started fussing with her nails and hair and had started acting distant. Callum would have noticed sooner if he hadn't been spending long hours at work. He had to take it on the chin on that one and take responsibility for leaving Hannah alone so much. He'd convinced himself their relationship would get on better footing once he secured their future and hadn't once stopped and asked himself if he was still happy in the relationship.

Payton cleared her throat, and he realized he'd momentarily zoned out. The bed frame made it easy to slide the mattress off. He picked up his side as Payton took hers. They arranged the makeshift bed toward the back wall to make sure no one tripped over it.

She stood up with her back straight and placed her hands on her hips, looking mighty proud of their accomplishment.

"You know what they say about teamwork," she said, practically beaming. Her smile had been too rare since they'd first met. It looked too good on her to be kept hidden, and he almost told her so. But this wasn't the right time for a compliment.

"I heard a lot of sayings about teamwork during my high school sports career. Which one are you referring to?" He cocked an eyebrow and paused.

"Makes the dream work," she quipped with a proud smile.

As corny as the saying was, he still smiled ear to ear in response.

PAYTON WASN'T SURE she could get used to sleeping in a home this grand. The guest suite was double the size of her apartment in Austin. Then again, that wasn't too hard to do. An involuntary shiver rocked her body at the memory of her place and what had happened there. She couldn't imagine stepping inside the apartment to pack everything up.

In her great-aunt's farmhouse, her belongings would feel different. She hoped the line wasn't a lie.

"I'll get cleaned up and let everyone know you're here," Callum said, causing her muscles to tense. He seemed to catch on when he added, "It's just the two of them. There are ranch hands and a foreman, but they don't come inside the main house. They'd be welcome, but they refuse."

The comment made her wonder if she should be here, either, despite Callum being clear she was more than welcome and wouldn't be in the way. All she really needed was a good night of sleep and a chance to catch her breath after a stressful day. Once she got her bearings, she could go home tomorrow and get back to fixing up the farmhouse. Staying busy physically with the repairs and mentally with her schoolwork kept some of the darkness at bay.

"I'll wait for you here," she said, wringing her hands together. She looked up to see Callum standing at the doorway, studying her. "I want to spend time with Atlas. We're fine."

"I won't be long," he said before disappearing down the hallway.

To say it had been a day would be the understatement of the week. Payton walked over to the mattress and then sat down on the floor.

"How am I doing so far?" she asked the sweet pup, who was snoring. He'd barely grown into his paws and had already been through so much. The shelter had said he came in emaciated, his fur in knots. The first signs of hope that he would be adoptable came early on when he took to the female volunteers. He would require special circumstances, but they'd said he could improve with training. Since Payton had no plans to allow any men in her life anytime in the near future, she hadn't seen a problem with taking Atlas home with her. Callum had her rethinking her stance.

So far, she and Atlas had done well together. She knew one thing was certain—she wouldn't have survived without him. Seeing him lying there, hurt, practically ripped her heart out of her chest. He was such a good boy who'd been mistreated. No more. He belonged to her now. Then again, she couldn't help but think he'd rescued her rather than the other way around.

Her thoughts drifted to the handsome Callum. He grew up in this house, so he clearly had more money than he could spend in a lifetime. And yet, he'd struck out on his own and started a logistics business in Houston. He had an air about him that said he'd built something successful from the ground up. She had a lot of respect for him and his accomplishments. But how could anyone who grew up like this still be so levelheaded and grounded? He was down-to-earth despite having a commanding presence. So much so, she didn't have to see him walk into a room to know he was there. She could feel his presence with the tiny hairs on the back of her neck that tingled when he was near.

At first, she'd been convinced he had to have a wife, but there was no ring on his left hand, and he hadn't mentioned anyone waiting at home in those early conversations. Payton wanted to know more about the Hayes family and especially Callum. They were going to be neighbors, so it probably wouldn't hurt to have a few friends. Since her great-aunt had trusted them, Payton would step out on faith and do the same.

Too bad Callum didn't plan to stick around.

Payton curled up on the floor near Atlas, using the mattress as a pillow. She bit back a yawn as another hunger pang reminded her that she still hadn't eaten. There was something about being at the Hayes family home that relaxed her. Before she realized it, she'd nodded off.

By the time Payton opened her eyes again, it was pitch-black outside, and a blanket had been placed over her. The lights were dimmed so she could see clearly as she sat up. Atlas snored, peacefully asleep, as her gaze landed on Callum. His head tilted to one side, and he was half sitting up on the couch.

Movement must have caught his eye, because his hand immediately came up to his face, like he was wiping sleep out of his eyes.

"How long was I out?" she asked, trying to get her bearings in the unfamiliar space. She took note of the fact that this was the first time in a week that she didn't wake up shaking, crying or screaming. The lingering effects of her ordeal recurred every time she let her guard down. Images of the Masked Monster haunted her dreams and gave her panic attacks before she opened her eyes.

"A few hours." Callum's deep, gravelly voice traveled over her. He sat up straighter. "I hope it's okay that I crashed here. I didn't want you to wake up in a strange home and have questions about whether or not an alarm had been set."

"That was thoughtful," she said. "I'm starting to worry about Atlas. He hasn't been outside to—"

"I took him out two hours ago when he woke up," Callum interrupted. "He did great. Peed on his own leg, but I got him cleaned up. He ate a little bit, not much. And he had plenty of water, so he might be peeing on his other leg the next time he goes out." He chuckled.

"He went outside with you?" she asked, more than a little shocked. It also freaked her out this had all happened while she was asleep and none of it woke her up.

"It probably helped that he's still sedated," Callum explained. "And he seems to be warming up to me, at least a little."

"You have such a calming presence," she said. On animals and on people, she thought but decided to keep that part to herself.

"Helps that I grew up on a ranch working with all kinds of furry creatures," he said. "I seriously doubt I would have gotten this far, though, without the sedation. He wasn't solid on his feet, which is the reason he wet his leg. Easy to clean up and better outside than on the bed."

"True. I'm still trying to figure out how I slept through all of it," she said and then gasped. "I just realized I have a paper due by 8:00 a.m." Why had she thought she could continue school and pull off a move?

"Then I better get some food and caffeine in you so you can focus," he said. "We can flip the lights on to make it brighter in here. Don't worry about making noise or waking anyone. The guest suite was built to be as far away as possible from the master suite and secondary bedrooms."

"Coffee sounds amazing right now, and I could probably eat this comforter," she admitted. "I don't want to leave Atlas."

"Stay right here, unless you want to work in the kitchen," he said.

"Here's fine," she quickly stated. "I can jump in the shower, then change into something more comfortable before you make it back."

"Do you have a preference on breakfast foods?" he asked, pushing up to standing. She didn't want to notice how his cotton T-shirt clung to his solid wall of muscles, highlighting every curve. Lights and coffee would go a long way toward shaking off the sexy image of him—an image she couldn't afford to let etch into her thoughts.

"Not really," she said. "Any kind of protein would be nice, since I missed dinner."

"Granny makes the most amazing skillet breakfasts. Eggs, sausage, potatoes. The works. She probably cooked the fatted calf for my homecoming. My mother was expecting my brothers and sisters to show, too. I'll heat something up and be right back," he said.

"As long as you're sure it won't disturb anyone," she said, pushing to standing.

He cracked a smile before disappearing down the hallway. The smile wormed its way into her heart, because truth be known, Callum Hayes was sex on a stick. And that was about as far as any of her past relationships had gone. As soon as things started heating up and it looked like there might be an attachment going on, she put on her running shoes and fled. Her parents' divorce had helped her realize that when people fell out of love, everyone around them ended up obliterated. How something that was supposed to be so wonderful and the be-all, end-all in life could turn into such hatefulness, as in her parents' case, had caused her to mistrust the institution of marriage, too.

Payton had never felt the need to have a man around to complete her. She wasn't broken or empty living on her own, no matter how much being around Callum made her think love might actually be a good thing. An honorable person who knew how to commit might make her feel differently. She was still a whole person, with or without the opposite sex in her life.

She left the bathroom door cracked as she stripped out of her clothes and then hopped into the shower. She wanted to be able to hear if Atlas woke up. It warmed her heart to no end to hear that he'd gotten along so well with Callum. Atlas trusted men about as much as she did. The statement wasn't exactly fair, she realized. But it wasn't too far off, either.

For a man like Callum, she might be willing to take another look at how she'd viewed relationships up until now.

## Chapter Eight

Callum heated up a couple of breakfast skillets as the coffee brewed. He was thankful his mother preferred an actual carafe of coffee rather than give in to one of those pod machines. He liked the smell of coffee, and this setup made it easier to have a second cup with very little fuss. Callum was all about less fuss in life.

He put together a tray and then headed back to the guest suite. Payton had been more tired than she'd realized last night, falling asleep while he cleaned up, changed and then had a conversation with his mother and granny. They'd be ecstatic at the possibility of meeting their new neighbor. He'd given them the basics: she lived alone and had adopted a new dog from a shelter. He'd explained that she'd inherited Beverly Baker's place and wanted to fix it up to make it livable again. When he'd told them about the living conditions, they'd clutched their chests.

It was his mother who seemed to catch on to the fact that he'd taken a shine to Payton. Her hopeful gaze had hit him in the wrong place. He wasn't in Cider Creek to find a wife. He would, however, help a neighbor. It was the ranching way, and just because he lived in the city now didn't mean he'd forgotten his upbringing.

As he entered the guest suite, he heard the spigot being turned off in the adjacent bathroom. Atlas was still sawing logs, which was a good sign. The best way for this guy to heal was to sleep. He'd been a good boy earlier and only tried to bite Callum a couple of times. He hadn't shared that information, because he didn't want Payton to feel bad or worry, and because Atlas wasn't putting a whole lot of effort into the attempts. He seemed to realize Callum was there to help, and the painkillers relaxed him enough for Callum to be able to work with him.

He set the tray down on the side table next to the couch.

"I can smell the food from in here," Payton said from the bathroom. He didn't need to picture her in there naked. He did. But he shoved the thought aside before it could take hold.

Callum had to smile at the situation. It was almost funny. He hadn't been with anyone since Hannah. He'd been too burned to think about sex and had stopped being a casual sex kind of guy years before. So, he should probably be happy that his libido was trying to rally. Under the circumstances, however, he told himself to calm down.

There was no doubt sex with Payton would knock his socks off. But she'd been through an ordeal that he wouldn't wish on his worst enemy, let alone a kind and compassionate person like her. She would need weeks if not months to heal and trust people again. Callum was leaving in a few days. He could see himself staying a week, tops. Logistically and in every other sense, nothing was going to happen between him and Payton.

Rather than sit there and stew about what could never be, he picked up a fork and stabbed it into some eggs. There were spinach, sausage and onions in the skillet bowl, and he couldn't wait to taste Granny's cooking again.

Payton emerged from the bathroom looking better than anyone had a right to in a jogging suit. Her slick, wet hair was pulled off her face in a ponytail, and her creamy skin practically shimmered in this lighting.

"The sun won't be up for a couple of hours," he said. "I trust you have time to get your paper written and turned in." Callum motioned toward the cup of fresh brew, proud he could provide a few comforts for Payton after all she'd been through.

"I keep thinking that trying to finish the semester is a mistake," she said, shaking her head. "And yet, I can't bring myself to drop the classes."

"Having schoolwork to focus on might not be the worst thing that could happen right now," he said. "At least while the police figure this out and catch the bastard."

"That's another reason to keep going," she admitted, taking the seat next to him. "In this weird way, it's almost like he wins if I drop out. I know that probably sounds juvenile, but—"

"I get it," he interrupted. "I do. Why let the jerk take everything away from you?"

"Right?" she agreed. "He has made me afraid of my own shadow, and I already hate that. If he takes school away from me, that just seems like I'm giving him too much. I've had to change up everything about my life. I gave up my apartment and my part-time job. The only thing left is my degree in social work."

Callum nodded in understanding.

"I had a fiancée recently," he said, unsure of why he was about to spill the details of his personal life. Maybe it was because he wanted Payton to know she wasn't alone out there in the land of awful things happening. "Apparently, she was having an affair right under my nose and I was none the wiser. The guy she was sleeping with was a new hire. I actually thought the guy was cool, so when she wanted to invite him over for dinner, I went along with it. Then, I open the door to his office one day, and there they are on his desk, going at it." He shook his head at the awful memory. "I told Trey to meet me in my office in fifteen after he cleaned up. All I wanted to do was get out of the building and never come back. Instead, I forced myself to stick out the rest of the day. Then, I got out of bed and showed up early the next morning, despite my future crumbling in that very building."

"How long had the two of you been together?" she asked with compassion in her tone.

"Five years," he told her. "There's no comparison in our situations. What you went through was horrific.

All I'm saying is that I understand the need to dig your heels in when something unfair happens to you."

The way she nodded and smiled felt like a bond of solidarity had just formed between them. Two people who knew what it was like to have someone damage them in some way.

"You didn't deserve to be treated like that," she said, taking a seat next to him and digging into the plate of food.

"Neither did you," he pointed out. "I've come to realize bad things happen to good people. The difference is good people rise up despite their circumstances."

She sat in silence for a long moment as though contemplating those words. He hoped they could help in some way. Too many times he'd heard someone wonder what they'd done to bring a bad event on them. The only real answer Callum could think of was that they'd been alive. It was as simple as that.

"I like that," she said. "My mother used to say people got what they deserved, and yet her actions never seemed to come back on her. She used people as much as she could and always seemed to skate free. Meanwhile, we had a neighbor who used to keep me in the early days of my parents' divorce, and she was the kindest lady you'd ever meet. She was robbed in the grocery store parking lot, and my mom said she brought it on herself by carrying too much cash. It just never resonated with me when my mother popped off like that."

"Agreed," he said, thinking her mother sounded

like a real piece of work. They hadn't delved into her family situation, but hearing this made him realize Payton was on her own. The family she had didn't seem like the type who would run to her aid unless there was something in it for them. "Bad things happen to everyone at some point. It's unavoidable. The trick is learning to truly live despite unexpected events."

Hearing himself say those words out loud also made him realize how silly he'd been in deciding to shut down the possibility of loving anyone ever again. It was an extreme punishment when he really thought about it, which didn't mean he could snap his fingers and open his heart up again. A little voice in the back of his mind picked that moment to point out the fact that he might not have been as in love with Hannah as he'd convinced himself. Being with her had become habit, and he could say, without a doubt, that he'd never felt with her anything close to the way he felt being around Payton right now. There were no fireworks going off in his chest the second their fingers touched, and there never had been.

Was it a rebound, or was this what he should have been expecting all along from relationships?

"Food for thought," Payton agreed, then looked down at her plate. She laughed, and it was a much-needed break from the seriousness of the subject.

Callum laughed, too. It was a nice feeling. He realized that since finding Hannah and Trey together, there'd been too little laughter in his life.

"I mentioned my ex and what she did," he started,

"but the truth is that I'm just as to blame for letting the relationship go south."

"You didn't cheat on her," Payton pointed out.

"No," he agreed. "Looking back, we'd both been unhappy in the relationship for a long time. We had a plan for our future, and I think we both felt like we needed to stick to it. Don't get me wrong, I'm not condoning her actions. They hurt like hell even if I'd fallen out of love with her years before."

Now he was realizing the word *love* might be a stretch for what they'd shared. There was a time when they'd enjoyed each other's company. Everyone changed, and she became more fixated on buying things, while he'd wanted to sock money away for their future. But money wasn't what split them apart. They didn't see life the same. Hannah would have lived at a crowded beach if given the opportunity. She could lie around all day and sunbathe, whereas he got bored after half an hour. He'd much rather go somewhere quiet and low-key. Hannah had wanted to eat out every night, while he was more of a homebody. He didn't mind doing the cooking. Women had just as many, if not more, skills than any man. Hannah didn't quite see it that way. She wanted to be taken care of, as she'd put it. The only part of the business she'd wanted any part of—it had turned out—was Trey. She wanted to spend her days sitting in a manicure chair, being pampered. When the subject of children came up, she'd wrinkled her nose and asked if they came with a nanny.

"I wanted an equal in every way," he finally said as

they took the last bites of food. "I wanted to be with someone who challenged me and helped me grow, not someone who was content to coast for the rest of our lives. Does that make sense?"

"A whole lot, actually," she admitted, causing his heart to stir. "Who wants to be with a plastic doll? I went on this date once with a guy who was incredibly good-looking, but he couldn't hold a conversation. It was the longest dinner date of my life."

"Exactly my point," he said. "I guess it would be one way of making a year feel like ten."

"Could you even imagine?" She rolled her eyes and laughed as she set her fork down.

Callum shouldn't allow himself to get too attached to the unexpected beauty. "I can put these away while you boot up your laptop and get to work."

He needed to leave the room and regain his balance before he fell head over heels for Payton.

*SHAKE IT OFF.* Payton would repeat those words until they became her mantra. The moment that had been happening between her and Callum—at least, she believed he felt it on his side, too—needed to stop, for both their sakes. Everything happening to her insides when he was close scared her.

What she needed to do was focus on writing a paper, get it turned in, and then see to Atlas's needs. Not necessarily in that order, since Atlas could wake at any time and need her. Renovations on the farmhouse could wait another day or two.

She picked up the coffee mug and took a sip. That

might be the best coffee she'd ever tasted, bar none. Then again, everything seemed better when Callum was around. She chalked her roller-coaster emotions up to recent events and did her level best to shove them aside before her imagination ran wild. Callum was an honorable person who was willing to help her out on a temporary basis. Confusing his generosity for anything else would do a disservice to them both.

Payton needed to stay in her lane.

Her laptop was charged and ready to go. At least she had that going for her. She settled into the couch and booted up. Thankfully, she had an outline to work from, so she wasn't starting from scratch. Her powers of concentration had been severely compromised since last week's ordeal. Refusing to give up and give in did feel good. In those first couple of days after the attack, she'd checked her cell phone a dozen times an hour, expecting the police to call with good news. None came. The few times she called to check on her case, she'd been told someone would contact her the minute there was news. She had half a mind to go after the bastard herself, but that would put her into the category of too stupid to live, so she wouldn't, no matter how tempting it was to try to put an end to this.

Landing at her great-aunt's place seemed more like fate now, like the universe was somehow nudging her toward a place to really be able to call home. *Think about the paper.*

Payton attempted to skim the outline four times before finally getting through it. Every time Atlas so much as snorted, she jumped to attention. *Squirrel.*

It didn't take much to distract her from the paper. She could sit here for the next four hours staring at the page, or she could smooth out the draft, turn it in and call it a day. At this point, all she wanted to do was pass the class. Any grade that got her the three hours of credit would be a win in her book. A semester shy of graduation, it would be a shame to waste all her hard work up to this point by quitting.

Pulling on every ounce of self-discipline she had left, she managed to smooth out the five-page, double-spaced paper on managing risk to safeguard children in half an hour. When she was finished, she glanced around, beaming, while searching for Callum. It took a second for her to realize he wasn't still in the room, less than that for disappointment to settle over her that he wasn't.

She logged into the system and uploaded her paper hours before the deadline. Satisfied that she'd at least made progress on her schoolwork, she closed down the computer. The urge to check her social media page and email was strong. The police had asked her to keep them open and to give their detectives access to see if the monster would try to stalk her online in order to figure out where she'd gone. She was the only one who knew his voice. It wouldn't be enough for a conviction. Any lawyer worth his degree would be able to pick her apart at a trial. A confirmation would, however, tell the police if they were working in the right direction or needed to move on from someone. She was invaluable to the investigation, they'd said.

Payton had shown them what little social media

she had. Her account was anemic at best. She'd never had time to take pictures and post them. She didn't have much of a life to post about, either. *Look, here is Payton studying for a test. Here she is again, making another cup of coffee for a customer.* She couldn't afford to go on a real vacation and cooked most of her own meals, which were of the basic variety. No one would accuse her of being a chef if they looked into her mostly bare food pantry. She knew enough of her way around the kitchen to survive. Now, if she could cook like Callum's grandmother, Payton would take pictures of those dishes and post them on social media. Those were something to look at, and the flavors were out of this world. Meanwhile, she was the queen of the peanut-butter-and-jelly-sandwiches-with-an-apple type meals. They got the job done.

Atlas whimpered in his sleep. In a heartbeat, she was up and by his side. She dropped down to her knees and smoothed her hand over his head, scratching the spot behind his ears that he loved.

Footsteps sounded from down the hallway, and her heart leaped into her throat. She reminded herself to breathe. The minute Callum came into view, she exhaled. Was she letting her guard down too easily around the handsome stranger?

## Chapter Nine

"I brought more coffee," Callum said to Payton, surprised to see her laptop closed and on the coffee table.

"I'll take it, but I'm done with the paper," she said as she soothed the sleeping animal.

"So fast?" he asked, not that it was any of his business. Not having work to focus on or a fiancée to appease gave him a surprising amount of free time. As it turned out, idle time was the devil's playground. He smiled at his own joke.

"I'm not saying it was great or that I should have turned it in so fast," she said, retrieving her coffee cup before handing it over for a refill. "I'm just saying that I'm finished. I'm realizing that sometimes completing a project has to be good enough."

"Do you want to try to get more sleep?" he asked.

"I haven't slept that deeply in a week—longer than that, if I'm honest, between my work and study schedule," she said before taking a sip of fresh brew. "I'm used to running on a few hours at night with naps every chance I get."

"You sound like a rancher during calving season,"

he said on a chuckle. He refilled his own cup and then took a seat. "Although starting a business is no joke when it comes to late nights and early mornings."

"I'd imagine you have to wear a whole mess of hats," she said, crossing her legs and hugging her knees into her chest as she sat next to Atlas.

"That would be correct," he said, thinking he'd never really shared much of the story with Hannah. She'd always seemed to get bored easily when he discussed anything about his work. "In the early days, I was known to hop on a truck and drive to get a shipment somewhere on time. Before I could hire employees, I answered my cell phone as though I was the receptionist." He cleared his throat and used a higher pitch. "Thank you for calling Hayes Logistics, how may I direct your call?"

Payton nearly fell over from laughing so hard. Seeing her with a genuine smile on her face after everything she'd been through was just about the most rewarding thing.

"You need more reasons to smile," he pointed out. "Your face lights up, and you somehow look even more beautiful."

She wiggled her eyebrows at him. Her laughter was as light as bubbles—until she snorted, which only made her laugh harder. Him, too.

"It's good to laugh," she said as she finally pulled herself together enough to manage a somewhat straight face.

"You don't sleep or laugh," he said, realizing how much her schedule and life sounded like his own recently. He hadn't slept well since Hannah had moved out. Actually, not since he caught her in the act. Expectations were a strange thing. Even though he could already admit their breakup was the best thing for both of them, it still stung worse than a bee sting in the face.

"Not much, no," she admitted. "I do drink copious amounts of coffee and smile at customers a whole lot."

"Speaking of which, do any of them stand out as possible suspects?" he asked, noting how quickly her smile faded when he brought the subject back to her case. His curiosity got the best of him, and he wanted to offer help if he could beyond letting her sleep in the guest room of his family home.

"His eyes stood out to me," she said, shaking her head. "I didn't wait on customers unless it was slow, so it's possible he came in and I didn't notice him. When I get into the zone making drinks, I'm all about those sticky labels on the cups. Caramel macchiato, vanilla latte, iced chai. My shop is one of the busiest, so we all specialize. Two people are working the cash register, and then I have another person calling out names once I hand them over. It's an assembly line."

"Sounds efficient," he said.

"We push through a whole lot of customers every hour. We have to be efficient, or we'd be eaten alive with a line out the door and spot checks by corporate," she said. "Our main goal is to keep the line inside the store. We rarely ever cleared it during my early-morning shifts. So, yes, he could have been there, watching. I rarely ever looked up when I got into a groove, and even when I did, it was from behind tall machines."

Her stalker could have been watching from outside for all they knew. He could have been inside and worn sunglasses. The sun was bright enough most winter days to pull them off without drawing attention.

"Leaves the door open for him," he said. "I'm guessing the front of the shop is all glass and there are most likely tables and chairs lining the sidewalk."

"Pretty standard setup for a coffee shop, right?" she asked, but it was more statement than question.

"Most that I've seen were in that format, from big chains to small mom-and-pops," he agreed. "Even if this person watched you from your home first, it wouldn't be difficult to follow someone around in a city like Austin, where there was foot traffic around almost 24/7 anywhere near campus."

"I'm head down and eyes focused on the sidewalk most of the time," she said. "Funny how it feels so safe in the downtown area because there are so many people out and about all the time. Summers are a different story altogether. The hustle and bustle slows down as most of the college kids head back home. You can finally rent a kayak on the weekend at Zilker Park, even though I never do."

"Strange how we notice all the things we should have done or that were available to us at different points in our lives," he said.

"All those missed opportunities," she agreed. "Being focused is a good thing. I mean, that's what I always tell myself." She paused for a beat. "And it is,

I think. Never relaxing or stopping to smell the pro-verbial roses is probably overboard."

"Except that you think you're building something for the future," he said. "And I'm realizing that the future never gets there. Or, when it does, it doesn't look the same as you'd imagined it to be. You know?"

"I do," she said with a whole lot of enthusiasm. "That's exactly what I'm trying to say. We get so caught up in making everything better for tomorrow that tomorrow never comes."

"We get caught in an endless loop," he said.

"And it's impossible to get off the merry-go-round," she stated, slapping her hand on her knee.

"The question is," he started, "how do we get off when it's time?"

"If I had the answer to that, I'd be a millionaire by now," she quipped. "Or at least better rested."

"I'm starting to think that slow and steady wins the race rather than one hundred percent focus on one task," he said. "My sole focus on building my busi-ness cost me a relationship."

Payton didn't immediately respond. He could tell by the way she sucked on her bottom lip that she was contemplating her answer. She seemed to throw cau-tion to the wind when she said, "I didn't and don't know your fiancée, and it's probably not my place to speak about your relationship."

She bit down on that bottom lip.

"But?" he asked, urging her to continue.

"It seems like a jerk move to sleep with someone in your company," she said. "Like she was slapping you in the face with it while you were there with your head down, working to build a future for the two of you." She put her hand up like she knew he was about to protest. "And I know. I get it. You worked too much. That's probably true. And it might have made you neglect the relationship. But, seriously? Did she have to sleep with someone who worked for you? *In* the building you own? If you ask me, she doesn't deserve you or the beautiful future you were trying to create."

He shook his head. "When you spell it out like that, she does come out the bad guy. And she certainly did her part to break me in half. Here's the other thing. Don't get me wrong, I was devastated for the future that I thought was gone. But somewhere in the back of my mind, I kept thinking how relieved I was that I didn't have to go through with marrying her."

"Did either of you ever bring up the subject?" she asked.

"I don't think either one of us knew how to do it without hurting the other one," he said.

"Well, she sure knew how to stab a knife in your chest," she argued. She was one hundred percent right.

"There had to be some vindictiveness in her actions. I'm not letting her off the hook," he said. "But talking about problems goes both ways, and I'm just as much at fault there."

Callum figured he'd learned his lesson and wondered if part of him hadn't realized early on that he and Hannah weren't a good match for the long haul.

Payton might be a different story. Everything he

was feeling about her was new, foreign and unexpected. Was it something that could last?

"I THINK YOU'RE taking the high road on this," she said, realizing it only made him more attractive—an attraction she couldn't let run its course, no matter how strong the pull. Even if she gave in to it for a little while, her brain would kick in at some point. "And I respect you for it."

"Thanks, but I like to own my mistakes. No one should get off too easily when they've done something wrong," he said. Based on what she knew about the handsome rancher–turned–business owner, he was hardest on himself. He seemed to be letting his ex off the hook.

He also made good points. There were two people in a relationship, and responsibility for making it work fell on both people's shoulders. Both had to be willing to talk through difficult patches and both had to *want* to be in it for the long haul. The latter could pose problems. She could see her relationship mistakes. The biggest one being she didn't believe two people could stay in love forever. Good role models were difficult to find. Her parents' marriage had been a disaster. They'd both remarried, but neither seemed particularly happy, just less miserable.

"It's only a matter of time before the shine wears off any relationship, right?" she said offhandedly, despite her instincts telling her that being in a relationship with Callum would be different. Instincts or wishes?

"My parents stayed married right up until the end for my father," he said. "I wasn't close with the man, since he was working most of the time, but he had a special bond with my mother. They loved each other. In fact, I'm not sure my mother ever recovered from the loss of her best friend."

"They had a long history together," she said. "Maybe meeting early in life, while people are still adaptable, makes the difference."

"You know, I asked my mom that question once," he said. "She said the only difference between her and Dad's marriage and those who divorced was that they made a decision every single day to stay together. They decided to work at it rather than give up. Said they'd been at a crossroad a few times when they didn't agree and couldn't see their way out of it."

"My parents could have used some coaching from yours," she said. "They handled their differences by tearing each other apart."

"I doubt my mother would claim to have had a perfect relationship with my father. He could be stubborn as a horse's backside when he wanted to be. I know they didn't always agree on his opinions on child rearing, but he deferred to her judgment most times. Now, my grandfather was a different story. He was as stubborn as a mule and mean on top of it," he said with a sharp sigh, and she could almost feel the pain fill the room as he exhaled. His tumultuous relationship with his grandfather obviously bothered him a great deal.

"Did she ever explain why he treated his grandchildren the way he did?" she asked, figuring there had to be some big reason. Folks rarely acted out for no reason.

He shook his head.

"And I never asked," he said. "Guess I figured that I shouldn't have to."

Callum shook his head again and cracked a dry smile.

"I'm starting to see a pattern here," he said. "Communication seems to be the key."

"It's easy to assume people know what we're thinking and feeling, and so easy to forget no one is a mind reader," she agreed. "I'm guilty of that myself, especially when school heats up and I don't come up for air until finals are over. People at work made it known that I could snap a little too quickly, and I always felt horrible about it after."

"Stress can do that," he said. "I was guilty of the same thing when I first started my business. With the weight of everything squarely on my shoulders, any problem could feel like a boulder when it was probably a rock."

"Can I ask how you overcame it?"

"I had a great employee who I wanted to groom to become my right hand. Here, I thought I was a great boss who shared the load with my employees, which also meant me being unfiltered when my temper got the best of me," he said. "To say I was the worst kind of leader wouldn't be inaccurate. Since I was the boss, there was no one to sit me down and tell me to cool off. Turns out, my few employees felt like they were walking on eggshells around me, which I learned when I landed a huge contract and two of my three employees walked out. They said that they wanted to be happy, and this big new job would only add to the stress around the office. My star employee couldn't get out the door fast enough."

"Clearly, your business survived," she pointed out.

"My one employee rounded up four people who were unemployed and couldn't find work," he said. "There was a reason no one wanted to hire them, and since my reputation as a boss wasn't exactly off to a good start, we were all each other had. I'm pleased to say those four people still work for me and are some of my top performers. Turns out, sometimes all anyone needs is a second chance to prove themselves. A year later, my former star employee came back and asked for a job. Said he'd be willing to start at the bottom if I'd give him a break."

"That's a huge compliment. I'm guessing you welcomed him back," she said.

"Funnily enough, I offered him a position at the bottom, and he took a pass. The talk was good, but he wasn't willing to back it up with the walk," Callum said on a chuckle.

"Giving him what he asked for didn't seem to make much difference," Payton stated.

"No. Because he wanted me to tell him how wonderful he was and that he was too good to start at the bottom again. If I'd had a position at the level he was looking at, I might have given him something better. But it was all I had, and I couldn't exactly bump someone out to make room," he said.

Atlas stirred, opening his eyes. He lifted his head and shook his head like he could break up the mental fog and get rid of the cone.

"Are you awake, buddy?" she asked, reaching over to scratch him behind the ears.

Light peeked through the plantation shutters on the windows. Had she really been talking to Callum that long? Hours had gone by. Time flew when she was with him, and she easily lost track.

"We can take him out, grab a few hours of sleep, and then I'll introduce you to my family," Callum said.

"Okay." Payton's pulse skyrocketed. After, she would have to face down the farmhouse across the street. She couldn't avoid going home forever.

## Chapter Ten

As Atlas took care of his business, his ability to walk improved after a couple of minutes on his feet. The cone of shame kept him distracted. He was still wary of Callum but stopped growling when the man got too close. All in all, a good sign of progress, and in a short amount of time. At this rate, he was going to steal Granny's title of animal whisperer.

Then, Callum and Payton curled up in their respective places and grabbed enough sleep to get through the day. Once they woke up, Callum led the way into the kitchen. Led a procession was more like it, with Payton walking closely behind him—he suspected she wanted the buffer—and Atlas hot on her heels.

Granny sat at the kitchen table nursing a cup of coffee while his mother emptied the dishwasher. The smell of eggs and bacon hung in the air, a sure sign they'd just finished eating.

"Mother, Granny," he started, "I'd like you to meet Ms. Baker's great-niece. This is Payton." He purposely didn't mention her last name, since she'd seemed nervous about revealing her identity. Maybe this way she would feel like she'd kept some small sense of her privacy intact.

"Hello, Mrs. Hayes," Payton said, taking a step out from behind Callum. Atlas stuck right by her side. "And Mrs...."

"Snide," Granny supplied.

"Ma'am," Payton said with a smile.

Mother turned around with an ear-to-ear smile.

"And who is this?" his mother asked as her gaze dropped to the dog.

"Atlas," Payton supplied. "I hope it's okay that he's in the house."

"Of course," she responded. "Is he okay?"

"Had a run-in with a wild hog," Callum supplied.

"Poor baby," his mother stated. Atlas didn't seem bothered being in the same room with the strange women. "Of course he's welcome. And I hope you'll call me Marla," his mother said to Payton, redirecting the conversation. She grabbed the dish towel that was splayed over her shoulder, set it on the counter and wiped her hands on her apron as she cut across the room. Rather than stick out a hand, she brought Payton into a hug.

Atlas started a low, throaty growl that caused Callum's mother to pull back.

"You're okay, boy," Payton soothed, and the animal responded by calming down.

"I probably should have asked first," his mother said. "I hope I didn't offend you with the hug."

"Hugs are good," Payton said with a warm smile and appreciation in her eyes. It was the reaction he'd hoped for. The two were going to be neighbors for the foreseeable future, and he wanted his mother and Payton to share a bond.

"This is Granny," he said, shifting focus. "Granny, I'd like to introduce you to Payton, and you've already met Atlas."

"Ma'am," Payton said, crossing the room. "Are you a hand shaker or a hugger?"

Granny practically jumped out of her chair, and the dog's ears didn't even perk up.

"I'll take a hug any day of the week," she said, meeting Payton halfway. As the two embraced, Callum's chest squeezed and Atlas lay down on the tile floor. When Granny pulled back, she studied Payton. He could have sworn he heard his mother whisper *traitor* in the background toward Atlas, her usual sense of humor shining through and causing him to chuckle.

"Thank you for the muffins yesterday," Payton said. "They were amazing."

"Any time," Granny said. Little did Payton know, a compliment to her baking was definitely the way to her heart. "And those aren't just words. I mean it. Now that Callum is moving home, I hope we'll see a lot more of you."

Callum bit his tongue as Payton's gaze flew toward him. He diverted his gaze—eye contact would be a bad idea—because it would give him away to his mother. From his peripheral vision, he saw her turn to the sink. He bit back a curse. His mother finding out this way wasn't ideal, but he was going to have to break the news to her at some point.

"He's already promised to help me with some renovations across the street," Payton said, saving the day with her comment. His mother sighed like she was relieved.

When he looked up, Granny plastered on a smile and held his gaze a second or two longer than usual. She was onto him. Thankfully, she didn't call him out.

"Oh good," his mother said, picking up on the conversational thread. She cleared her throat. "Callum is handy with a hammer, saw and pretty much every other tool. He'll be great help."

"Is there a lot of work to be done?" Granny asked.

"The place is pretty much in need of top-to-bottom renovation," Payton said. "I've been saving a little money since my great-aunt left me the house, but it'll still take a while with all the updates that need to happen."

Granny's smile of approval meant she took it to mean he would be there for the duration of the project. There was no harm in him being away from work for a couple of weeks, maybe a month. If he applied himself and gathered a few extra hands, he could probably have Ms. Baker's old place fixed up well before Christmas. As far as money went, he had more than enough and would offer to do the work pro bono.

"It's getting colder outside," Granny said.

"That might speed up my timeline on certain projects," Payton admitted. "But I can only go as fast as my budget allows."

"Which is understandable," Mother said a little too eagerly. She wouldn't want the project to end too quickly, because she seemed to think Callum volunteering to help was a sign. Had she been wondering whether or not he'd be able to walk away from a business he'd built from the ground up? She had to realize how important his company was to him, not to mention all the employees he would be abandoning.

For the first time since he'd arrived yesterday morning, he realized his mother might have suspicions about his intention to move back home. To be fair, he'd made no promises. She'd made the request for all the siblings to come home, and she hadn't asked a whole lot of questions as to whether or not anyone was ready. The instructions had been simple: come home and take his rightful place.

"You have beautiful red hair," Payton said to his mother, who smiled at the compliment.

"I have to give the color a little boost these days," his mother said with a little skip in her step. She did still have thick, wavy shoulder-length hair.

"Will you stay around in Cider Creek once you fix up the old house, or do you plan to sell?" Granny asked, reclaiming her seat and picking up her coffee mug.

"That's none of our business," Mother intervened with a scolding look aimed at Granny.

"It's okay," Payton said, waving it off like the question was no big deal. "Right now, I'm just trying to get through my semester at school and fix the place up enough to be able to sleep in a proper bedroom.

The project is pretty ambitious and money is tight, so I'm prepared for it to take a while. To be honest, I haven't given much thought to what I plan to do once I graduate. I had an idea at one time, but things changed unexpectedly, and now I'm here." She shrugged. "Sometimes life has other ideas despite all my careful planning."

"Sounds like you'll be busy," Granny said. "I'll be sure to send Callum over with food so you can stay focused on school and the renovation."

"You really don't have to—"

"Nonsense," Granny interrupted. "It would give me something useful to do and I would enjoy it. I'm sure I'll be cooking and baking a whole lot more as my grandkids return. One more person won't make a hill of beans' difference in how long I'm in the kitchen."

Callum seriously needed to have that talk with his mother and Granny. Telling them no one planned to come home was going to be more difficult than he'd originally believed. The last thing he wanted to do was kill the spark in Granny's eyes at talk of their return.

He bit back a sigh, realizing he had his work cut out for him.

PAYTON COULD SEE tension building in Callum's face at the talk of him sticking around town and his brothers and sisters coming home. Her heart hurt for all parties involved at the conversation he needed to have. It sat over his head like a heavy gray rain cloud.

"I look forward to meeting the whole family," Payton said when nothing else came to mind.

"You'd be welcome to stay here while you get the house up to code," Callum's mother said in a surprise move.

"I couldn't inconvenience you like that and, besides, I have no real timeline for—"

"It wouldn't be any trouble at all," his mother piped in. "The forecast is calling for a cold snap to come in tonight. I wouldn't sleep a wink if you went back before the place was ready."

The thought of spending several nights—let alone weeks or months—under one roof with Callum sent her stomach into a somersault routine. She tried to keep her breathing steady and even so she wouldn't give herself away. Her body had a mind of its own, because her pulse raced and her skin goose bumped.

"I didn't realize weather was headed this way," Payton said in an effort to keep her mind off Callum. "I haven't checked the forecast in days."

"You don't have to take Mother up on her offer," Callum said. "She would understand if you felt more comfortable sleeping across the street."

Disappointment caused her shoulders to deflate.

"Having said that, I agree wholeheartedly that you should stay here. It'll be better for Atlas to stay warm, and last time I checked, the heat wasn't working across the street," he said. "We would love to have you here."

He didn't outright say it would be safer for her, too, but the look that passed between them helped her read his thoughts. With Atlas down for the count for the next couple of days, possibly weeks, she had no security aside from the shotgun. The minute she fell asleep, she would be vulnerable.

"If you're sure I won't be in the way," she started. "Maybe just until Atlas is feeling better."

"Not at all," Callum's mother said almost immediately. "In fact, I would love having another female in the house."

"Plus, it'll give us a chance to get to know each other better," Granny interjected. She clapped. "It's settled then, right? You're moving into the guest room."

Payton smiled and nodded. She needed to put Atlas's needs first anyway, and being here was much better for him while he recovered. There were more people to look after him who had a whole lot more experience with animals than she did. Having people around who knew what they were doing would be a nice change of pace.

Glancing over at Atlas, she realized he'd made himself at home real quick in the Hayes household, especially on the cool tile in the kitchen. Poor guy. He was being a good sport about wearing the cone of shame.

"Sit down," Granny urged. "Have a cup of coffee."

"Where are my manners?" Callum's mother... Marla asked. "Please, sit. What can I get for you?"

"I'm okay, but Atlas needs to be fed," she said, glancing around for a bowl that would work.

"I got this," Callum said, immediately jumping to

work. He moved over to a cabinet on the opposite wall and pulled out a couple of baking dishes. He put water in one and set it on the floor near Atlas, who didn't seem as bothered by Callum's presence. "I brought his food in last night and put it on the back porch. I'll be right back."

She should probably be nervous at being alone with Callum's mother and grandmother, except that they were the warmest, kindest people she'd ever met. His mother was on the shorter side and had a gorgeous head of fiery red hair. A few freckles dotted her cheeks and nose. For someone who was tiny, she seemed mighty. She had a quiet strength about her that Payton couldn't help but admire. Granny was a character, and she seemed to know it. All her hair was coarse and gray, in a loose bun on top of her head. She wore a flannel dress that probably doubled as a nightgown, socks that were folded in half and slippers. There was something cozy about them both, like sitting near a roaring campfire on a cold night. The motherly hugs from both women had caused Payton to stiffen at first. She'd never been hugged like that before, and the feeling had been foreign until she relaxed into it.

"Can you stay for coffee while Callum fixes breakfast for Atlas?" Granny asked.

"One more cup couldn't possibly hurt." She hadn't finished the last one anyway. In fact, her cup was probably still on the table in the guest suite. She needed to remember to bring it back to the kitchen. "But I can get it myself."

"Nonsense," Marla said, waving like she was swatting a fly. "Soon enough, you'll be considered family and therefore required to get your own. For now, enjoy being a guest."

Payton couldn't help but laugh.

"Come sit by me," Granny said, patting the chair next to her.

How could Payton not comply with a sweet request like that one? She walked over as Atlas stood up and followed. His movements were awkward, and he kept trying to crane his neck around to lick his injury, to no avail. But she had to give him credit for hanging in there. After breakfast, she could give him something for the pain.

Payton joined the older woman.

"I hope you'll call me Granny," she said.

"Deal," Payton stated. "It would be an honor."

"I don't want to step on any toes with your grandparents," Granny said with a twinkle in her blue eyes.

"No worries there," she responded without missing a beat. "I don't know them. My mother didn't speak to her parents, who split up years ago, and my father's parents passed away when I was too little to remember much about them."

Granny reached over and covered Payton's right hand with hers.

"Well, you're not alone now," the older woman said with a smile warm enough to melt a glacier during an Alaskan winter.

Payton blinked back tears as she thanked Granny quietly.

Atlas watched Callum as he filled his food bowl. He warmed and then poured in a little chicken broth, saying it might be easier on his stomach. The way Callum had with animals, especially her complicated dog, impressed her. She'd heard dogs were good judges of character. And even a broken spirit like Atlas seemed to sense the goodness in the room.

"When he's finished, we can head across the street," Callum said.

She nodded, but the thought of leaving struck her like a physical blow. This was the first place she'd truly felt like she fit in, in longer than she could recall.

## Chapter Eleven

"What would you like to start on today?" Callum asked Payton after his mother and Granny cleared out of the kitchen and they had the room to themselves. The dog hadn't tried to bite him even once while Callum fed him. There was hope, and that was all he needed.

"It would be nice to have a decent kitchen to work with, but the bedroom has to take priority," she said after a thoughtful pause. "In good news about the kitchen, the appliances all work, surprisingly, and I'm pretty certain they're original. Not having to replace them might help me get the kitchen up soon after the bedroom."

"They don't make 'em like they used to," he said, and she seemed eager to agree.

"The wood flooring is in need of repair. There are loose planks. I probably need to refinish them, too. I'm guessing that I can google it and rent a machine," she said. "The cabinets can use refacing or, at the very least, repairing, sanding and repainting."

He nodded. That was all doable.

"I can do better than renting a machine," he said, fishing his cell phone out of his pocket. "I know a guy who'll do the job for us for a six-pack."

"No way," she countered, not hiding her shock.

"He owes me a favor, and I've never had a chance to collect," he said. "While we have him, though, I'd like to do the whole place."

"That sounds like too big of a job for a favor," she argued, and it was easy to see based on her expression and resistance that she wasn't used to people doing anything for her. That was about to change.

"I grew up here and have a whole lot of connections," he said. "Refinishing the floors on your own with school and Atlas would be a bigger challenge than you probably realize. We can start today by prepping the area as much as possible. Dust will get everywhere, so I'd advise covering cabinets with plastic, etc."

"I can do that," she agreed. "If you're sure about the favor."

Callum cracked a smile. She really had no idea how it worked in a small ranching community. Hardy Jenkins didn't just owe Callum a favor—Hardy owed Callum his life. Now he had a thriving home renovation business, along with a wife and a kid. Callum would know, because he received an annual Christmas card from the family along with a personal note from Hardy, who always closed by asking Callum if there was anything Hardy could do for him.

He fished out his cell phone, fired off a text and got an almost immediate response.

Send the address and I'll have a crew there tomorrow.

Callum responded with the information, and before he could put his cell phone away, he got a message from Gregory. After reading it, he smiled at Payton.

"Good news," he said. "Your belongings have made it to storage."

A picture came in, so he moved over next to Payton where she stood at the granite island and then tilted the screen so that she could see.

"That's a miracle," she said practically under her breath. When she turned her head and caught his gaze, the air in the room charged with electricity. He could already feel the temperature rising in the space around them, as though someone had turned on the heat.

Her eyes sparkled with something that looked a whole lot like need. This was the moment that Callum probably should have taken a step back or away and refocused. Did he? No. Instead, he watched her pulse pound at the base of her throat and slicked his tongue across his bottom lip. His throat suddenly dried up as though he'd licked a glue stick, and all he could concentrate on was the clean, lilac-scented fragrance in her hair.

His resolve wasn't helped one bit when she pushed up to her tiptoes, closed her eyes and then kissed him.

Callum took in a deep breath, which only served to fill his senses with lilac. He brought his hand up to her chin and then tilted her face toward his for better access. And then he dipped the tip of his tongue to her lips, which parted for him. All rational thought flew out the window as she bit down on his bottom lip. His breath quickened, his pulse skyrocketed and one word echoed in his thoughts…*more*.

He wanted more. More of Payton's silky skin against his. More of her body flush with his. More of *her*.

Was this a bad idea? His heart argued that something that felt so right couldn't possibly be wrong. Rationally, he knew she was different from Hannah, which was true. Payton had the ability to shatter him. Whereas Hannah had only embarrassed him and hurt his pride. He could see that more clearly now. The two of them had been together for years, and being with her had become habit. The breakup had a been a loss of what the future could have been. However, he was beginning to see that ultimately neither one of them would have been happy in the long run. Hell, they had been miserable in the short term.

But Payton was different. Until he knew exactly what that meant, he needed to slow his roll.

Pulling on all his willpower, he took a half step back. She muttered an apology and something that sounded a lot like her promising it wouldn't happen again.

"There's no need to say you're sorry for doing something we both wanted," he said as she brought her hand to her lips like she'd never been kissed like that before. A knot formed in his chest at the thought of never doing it again.

Right now, it was best not to try to predict the future. Instead, he wanted to forget the memory of the kiss before it burned into his thoughts and took hold.

"You're a great person, Callum," she said, locking gazes with his in a surprise move. "And that kiss was right up there with the best of my life, so, no, I don't regret it one bit." She paused for a beat. "But I know myself, and the minute anything starts to get serious, I bolt. As much as I want to believe it would be different with you, past behavior is always the best predictor of the future. Right?" It was more statement than question. "Since I'd really like to be friends, I'm hoping we can forget that happened. Let's rewind and go back to where we were before."

"Sounds like a plan to me," he said, knowing full well that he couldn't possibly dismiss a kiss so intense that it almost made him forget his own name. She'd made several good points, and he wasn't in the market for a serious anything right now. Not after the number Hannah had played on him. One look into Payton's eyes said her mind was made up on the subject. She left no room for doubt that she would only walk away from him anyway. Callum wasn't stupid. He knew Payton would never cheat, but that didn't mean she wouldn't break his heart.

"Good," she said, but her tone held a whole lot of hurt and uncertainty that she tried to cover with a cough. He figured it was best to leave it alone.

"Should we get to work?" he asked, holding out his arm for her to grab on to.

She took the offering.

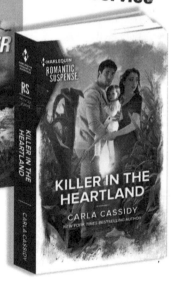

## Get up to 4 FREE FABULOUS BOOKS in your welcome box!

To thank you for being a loyal reader we'd like to send you up to 4 FREE BOOKS, absolutely free when you try the Harlequin Reader Service.

Just write "YES" on the Loyal Reader Voucher and we'll send you your welcome box with 2 free books from each series you choose plus free mystery gifts! Each welcome box is worth over $20.

Try **Harlequin® Romantic Suspense** and get 2 books featuring heart-racing page-turners with unexpected plot twists and irresistible chemistry that will keep you guessing to the very end.

Try **Harlequin Intrigue® Larger-Print** 2 books featuring action-packed stories that will keep you on the edge of your seat. Solve the crime and deliver justice at all costs.

Or **TRY BOTH** and get 2 books from each series!

Your welcome box is completely free, even the shipping! If you continue with your subscription, you can look forward to curated monthly shipments of brand-new books from your selected series, always at a discount off the cover price! Plus you can cancel any time.

So don't miss out, return your Loyal Readers Voucher today to get your Free Welcome Box.

*Pam Powers*

# LOYAL READER
# FREE BOOKS VOUCHER
# WELCOME BOX

▼ DETACH AND MAIL CARD TODAY! ▼

## YES! I Love Reading, please send me a welcome box with up to 4 FREE BOOKS and Free Mystery Gifts from the series I select.

Just write in "YES" on the dotted line below then return this card today and we'll send your welcome box asap!

➡ _ _ _ YES _ _ ⬅

Which do you prefer?

☐ **Harlequin®
Romantic
Suspense**
240/340 HDL GRTY

☐ **Harlequin
Intrigue®
Larger-Print**
199/399 HDL GRTY

☐ **BOTH**
240/340 & 199/399
HDL GQ93

FIRST NAME | LAST NAME

ADDRESS

APT.# | CITY

STATE/PROV. | ZIP/POSTAL CODE

EMAIL ☐ Please check this box if you would like to receive newsletters and promotional emails from Harlequin Enterprises ULC and its affiliates. You can unsubscribe anytime.

HI/HRS-622-LR_LRV22

**HARLEQUIN® Reader Service** —Here's how it works:

Accepting your 2 free books and 2 free gifts (gifts valued at approximately $10.00 retail) places you under no obligation to buy anything. You may keep the books and gifts and return the shipping statement marked "cancel." If you do not cancel, approximately one month later we'll send you more books from the series you have chosen, and bill you at our low, subscribers-only discount price. Harlequin® Romantic Suspense books consist of 4 books each month and cost just $5.49 each in the U.S. or $6.24 each in Canada, a savings of at least 12% off the cover price. Harlequin Intrigue® Larger-Print books consist of 6 books each month and cost just $6.49 each in the U.S. or $6.99 each in Canada, a savings of at least 13% off the cover price. It's quite a bargain! Shipping and handling is just 50¢ per book in the U.S. and $1.25 per book in Canada*. You may return any shipment at our expense and cancel at any time by calling the number below — or you may continue to receive monthly shipments at our low, subscribers-only discount price plus shipping and handling.

"Let's do this," she said on an exhale.

Callum led her outside as Atlas followed. He walked a whole lot better now that he'd eaten. Callum had placed the dog's pain pill in the bowl of food and was pleased when he noticed the bowl was completely empty on his way out of the kitchen.

As they neared the truck, Payton stopped and looked at him.

"We're okay, right?" she asked, and there was so much concern in her voice that he decided she was just as freaked out about what had transpired between them as he was.

"Solid on my side," he reassured. Everything about Payton was different, and he wanted to get to know her better before he threw his fool heart her way. The annoying voice in the back of his mind said it was too late. He ignored it. What did that voice know anyway?

PAYTON HOPED SHE hadn't just ruined a friendship before it could get off the ground. She already cared deeply for Callum Hayes and wanted their relationship to last. She questioned whether or not she'd been smart to act on impulse—an impulse that seemed to have a mind of its own. For once, she'd followed her heart and quieted her thoughts.

And now, she could only pray she hadn't made it awkward with her one true friend in Cider Creek. Facing down the farmhouse without Callum wasn't something she wanted to do. She'd come to need him in a short time, and Payton had never needed anyone except herself. His family had been so sweet to make her feel welcome and included. She'd gotten caught up in it all. That was it. Plus, face it, Callum was gorgeous. He was intelligent, compassionate and caring. His touch with animals was swoonworthy. What was it about a man who could tame a wild animal that made her pulse pound?

She'd been on a roller coaster, and he had offered a respite. This seemed like a good time to remind herself not to get caught up in her emotions again. Besides, friendship was all she could handle right now anyway. Anything else would short-circuit her.

Last night had been the first in a week that she didn't wake up with tremors after a nightmare. She had no plans to ruin it by crossing a line that never should have been crossed in the first place.

"Hey, boy, are you ready for today?" she asked Atlas as they neared Callum's truck.

His response was to do his business right next to her. So, yes, he was now ready for work. She almost laughed out loud at the timing.

Callum did laugh.

"We'll swing by the barn in order to get supplies," he said. "How is Atlas with other animals?"

"As far as I know, he's only afraid of men," she said. "I'm thinking he'll be fine."

"We'll know in a few minutes," he said.

"The grounds, this land is absolutely beautiful," she said as she glanced around. The yard—if it could be called that—surrounding the home was immaculate. Tire swings hung from the trees, and there was a fire pit surrounded by six white Adirondack chairs behind the two-story estate. The home itself looked like something out of the '80s show *Dallas*. It was stately and grand, and all the things that came to mind when imagining what the home of millionaire cattle ranchers might look like. The house was white with black shutters and had a massive porch out front. It sprawled across two levels in front of a long drive. The roof was black, and the entire front yard was encircled by wood fencing. Make no mistake about it, though, security here was top-notch. Barely noticeable cameras hung from trees. A long driveway would make it impossible to surprise the Hayeses. Plus, there was a security gate to get through in the first place, staffed by a live person who most likely had a military background, based on the haircut of the attendant she'd seen last night.

There was an impressive set of white barns in back of the home. They were far enough that it made sense to drive.

Callum helped Atlas into the back seat of his king-cab pickup before opening her door.

"I do realize that you can open the door for yourself, but manners are ingrained in me, so I apologize if you take offense," he said.

"I'm personally glad that chivalry isn't dead," she said with a smile.

"Good, because I like holding doors open for you," he admitted.

"And I could get used to being spoiled," she responded. There was a sense of honor in Texas that she'd never experienced anywhere else in the few times she'd traveled out of the state. And she figured there was some ranching or cowboy honor code at work in the way she was treated by locals. She knew the difference right away and always appreciated when someone offered to hold a door or extend a hand while she exited a vehicle. Honor was becoming too rare in a world that seemed to want to see how fast it could make time fly.

She thought back to her old neighbor, who could use a few lessons in chivalry.

Payton's cell buzzed, surprising her, because very few folks had been given her new number. A call from an Austin area code made her heart thump against her ribs. She answered.

"Ma'am, this is Detective Aaron from Austin PD," he started. "Is this a good time?"

If he had new information about the case? Yes.

"I can talk," she said after confirming her identity.

"We have a suspect in custody and would appreciate it if you could come down and see if you can identify the perp in a lineup," he said.

Her heart thundered now.

"What is it?" Callum asked before he shut the door.

"They think they have him," she whispered before returning to the call. "How soon do you need me to get there?"

# Chapter Twelve

Callum claimed the driver's seat, cranked on the engine and waited. A change of plans brewed, and he had a strong feeling based on listening to this side of the conversation they were about to head out on a different course.

Payton ended the call.

"The new deputy in charge of the investigation is sending over an address," she said. "You can drop me off at my car across the street. Doesn't look like I'll be working on the farmhouse today."

Driving round trip to Austin would take up most of the day.

"If we leave now, we'll get there before lunch," he said, not once considering letting her do this on her own. "We can be back by supper."

"You've already done so much for me," she countered. "Not to mention Atlas. I can't ask that of you."

"You didn't," he pointed out. "I wholeheartedly volunteered."

"Are you sure about this?" she asked. "I'm a lot right now, and you have other obligations. You've been so generous already that I don't know how I'll ever repay your kindness, which you'll tell me is not the point, but still."

Callum sat there, arms folded across his chest, listening as her words almost tripped over each other trying to get out. She spoke fast, like if she slowed down she might change her mind midsentence.

"Believe me when I say that I wrote the book on not wanting to be indebted to anybody," he started, trying to find the right words. He sat for a moment with the engine idling. "I'm here in Cider Creek and will be for at least a couple of weeks. I have a feeling that I'm going to have to let my mother down easy—hurting her in any way is not what I have in mind, but it can't be helped without rearranging my life. Helping you actually makes me feel like I'm not a completely selfish jerk. That being said, I understand if you need to face this on your own. Either way, I'm here. Tell me what you want and not just what you think you should say."

"If I'm being totally honest, I don't want to do this alone," she began before fidgeting in her seat. "I'm also starting to develop feelings for you that are so unfamiliar they scare me."

He could relate to that last part.

"Since I don't do long term with anyone, I'd like to be friends, because I would very much like for you to be in my life," she admitted. "And I sure as hell can use a friend right now."

"Friendship sounds good to me," he said, realizing they were rowing the same boat. Considering his breakup and the bad taste it had left in his mouth, logic said to pull back and give this thing time to figure itself out.

Rather than dig too deep in that pit, he put the gearshift in Reverse as her cell indicated a text had come in. She rattled off an address that he logged into his GPS before shifting directions.

"We can eat lunch in Austin," he said, navigating down the long, paved driveway.

"There's a little place by my apartm—"

She stopped midsentence as though suddenly realizing she didn't live there any longer. "I hope they have the bastard locked up so they can throw away the key."

"There's only one way to find out," he said, "and we're doing it."

"I don't know if I can positively identify him," she said on a frustrated sigh. "I remember his blue eyes that turned cold, and the sound of his voice is forever etched in my brain. But that's all I have."

"It's more than they had to work with before you," he reassured.

"That's true," she said as she shivered. "The thought of facing him again, seeing those eyes or hearing that voice—"

She shivered again.

"I'll be with you, standing beside you, ready to catch you if you fall," he said. "He can't hurt you again."

Payton folded her arms across her chest, rubbing

them like she was trying to stave off the cold despite the cab being warm.

"I won't let him," she finally said after a few beats of silence. "He won't catch me off guard this time. I have his number now and know exactly what kind of man he is."

Her anger was good, but that didn't stop him from wanting to reach across the cab and pull her close, protect her. She was strong, and he admired her for it. No one was an island, though. Leaning on others for support didn't make someone weak. He should probably take his own advice, because he'd folded inside himself to deal with Hannah's betrayal—a betrayal that had struck harder than a physical blow.

"I know that you can do all this on your own," he started. "I'd still like to be here for you. What I went through with Hannah is nothing like what you're facing, so I'm not comparing the two by any means. However, I do know what it's like to go inside yourself and not reach out for help. I can be the worst when it comes to bucking up or taking it on the chin. It's something I'm working on. It's good to let people in and let them help—and so much easier to tell that to someone else than actually do it for yourself. But I'm here in any capacity you need me to be, including but not limited to friend."

"It means a lot to hear you say that, Callum," she said, and he could tell by her tone that she meant every word.

"Whatever is happening between us doesn't need a definition for it to be real to me," he continued. "You want me as a friend? You got it. You need something more? You got that, too. We don't have to promise forever to be here for each other right now." He'd learned the hard way intentions and words didn't always lead to forever anyway.

"Good," she said. "Because what I feel for you is definitely stronger than friendship, and I don't have the emotional bandwidth to try to figure it out right now."

She unbuckled, scooted over and then repositioned herself in the middle seat. Then she leaned her head on his shoulder.

Payton seemed to mentally switch gears as he navigated onto the highway. "There's going to be a lineup."

"He won't know who is on the other side of the glass," Callum pointed out before realizing the error in his logic.

"He has to know it's me," she said with a shiver.

"Not for certain. There could have been witnesses. Someone seeing him run away from the building or a tenant," he surmised. The probability was that the perp would assume it was her, considering she was the only one who'd escaped death. There was at least a possibility that it wasn't.

"True," she agreed without much enthusiasm as she leaned in a little closer. He liked the fact his physical touch seemed to offer some reassurance when his words fell short.

The rest of the ride to Austin was spent in companionable silence, a sharp contrast to the way Hannah always seemed to need to fill the void with words. She would go on mindlessly while he focused on the road and got lost in his own thoughts. All she'd needed was the occasional *uh-huh* to keep going in a conversation he'd long since checked out of. In the early days, he'd enjoyed the company after isolating himself for so long. The fact that Hannah could talk endlessly about something as trivial as her nails hadn't been a problem. His brain was usually fried after working long hours anyway, so he didn't mind the distraction. They had decided to take their relationship slow, and it wasn't until she'd moved in with him that he'd started seeing warning signs. Once he put the ring on her finger and made the promise, a few more things slipped. If they'd happened early on in the relationship or all at once, he would have seen the red flags for what they were. His relationship with Hannah had changed over time, and he'd been too busy to take stock.

Hannah and Payton couldn't be more different. She seemed content to sit there with him, with no need to fill the air with empty words. And the contrast between them didn't end there. Payton was focused on finishing her education, whereas all Hannah had seemed concerned with was having someone around who had money in the bank. Payton made her own way in life, whereas Hannah had said she always needed someone around.

In some ways, Callum figured Payton was shoring up her strength for the task ahead right now. Taking solitude in the silence. When he really thought about it, this was the first time she was going back to Austin since the whole ordeal had happened, and facing the town again had to be stressful. She hadn't wanted to so much as step inside her apartment again, and he didn't blame her one bit.

They pulled into the parking lot of the main substation where the perp was being held. Payton sat straight up and picked at her cotton T-shirt.

"I just realized I'm still wearing a jogging suit," she said. "I probably should have dressed up a little more for this."

"You look amazing to me," he said and could hear the frog in his own throat.

"What about Atlas?" she asked. "They won't let him inside."

"I can stay with him, and I'll be right here when you get back," he said. "He probably needs to stretch his legs after being in the truck for a few hours. We'll wait right here for you."

"Promise you won't leave?" she asked before shaking her head. "Never mind. I trust you to do what you say. You aren't the type to go back on a promise. My nerves are just kicking up, but seriously, I'll be fine."

"You're one of the strongest people I've ever met," he said. "It's okay not to be one hundred percent at all times. It's okay to be unsure and a little bit shaky. And it's okay to need a few minutes before facing the darkest moment of your life."

Payton made eye contact and, instantly, he could see that she understood and appreciated what he was

saying. It seemed to resonate as she took in a fortifying breath.

"Here goes nothing," she said before exiting the
vehicle and making the short walk to the front door.
Inside, she would be greeted by law enforcement officers. He had no doubt they would take good care
of her.

Rather than sit here and twiddle his thumbs, he
exited the vehicle and managed to help Atlas out of
the back seat. The pain medication was helping with
Atlas's nerves. He only snapped at Callum once, and
the attempt was half-hearted.

Callum would take the progress. When it came to
Payton, he had no easy answers, no matter how much
he wanted to be able to make promises—promises he
had no idea if he could keep.

PAYTON OPENED THE glass door that led into a small
lobby. A counter separated her from the desk sergeant, who immediately looked up from the computer
screen the minute she stepped inside.

"How may I help you, ma'am?" the older gentleman asked. He was a solid six feet tall, thin, with a
sheet of gray on top of his head. Tufts of gray hair
peeked out of his dark blue, solid-colored shirt. The
top button of his collared shirt was unbuttoned, and
his tie was loose. He immediately fixed the situation,
buttoning up and tightening his tie as he met her gaze.

"My name is Payton Reinert. I'm here for the
lineup," Payton explained as her pulse kicked up a
couple of notches, threatening to rocket into another

stratosphere. She took a few calming breaths and continued, "I received a call from a detective."

The desk sergeant's eyebrows drew together.

"Did the detective mention his name?" he asked.

"Yes, he said his name was Detective Aaron," she supplied.

"I'm sorry, ma'am, but we don't have anyone by that name here," he said. His fingers danced across the keyboard. "I can look to see if you have the wrong substation."

"He texted this address to me," she said as she felt the blood drain from her face.

"Would you like to sit down, ma'am?" the sergeant asked.

"Yes." Payton took a couple of steps back, feeling for the wall. "My friend is outside with my dog. Is there any way that he can come in?"

"We can take a walk outside," the sergeant said.

"No, I can't. *He's* out there. He found me." Payton reached for the wall behind her and then leaned against it for support. A string of curses came to mind as she regained her composure. She hadn't thought to verify the so-called Detective Aaron was a real person.

"Who is out there? Your friend or someone else?" the sergeant asked, studying her like he was evaluating her mental capacity.

"Look up Payton Reinert. You can find my case in the computer," she said, wondering how on earth he'd gotten ahold of her number. Did he know someone in law enforcement? Have access to files? "I'm a victim of the Masked Monster."

Those words got the sergeant's feet moving back behind his counter. He banged out a few words on the computer before muttering one of the swear words she'd just thought.

"My friend is outside with my dog," she repeated. "Can we bring them both inside?"

"What does he look like?" the sergeant asked. "I'll wave him in."

She rattled off Callum's description as well as Atlas's. The two couldn't be missed, especially when they were together.

The sergeant nodded before making a beeline for the door. He didn't go all the way outside. Instead, he wedged himself in the frame of the glass doors and waved his arm until he seemed to catch Callum's attention.

There were half a dozen questions circulating in Payton's mind. He was being arrogant inviting her to a police substation, letting her know that he could operate right underneath the cops' noses.

The Masked Monster had an ego. It was clear that he was frustrated with her for being the one to get away. Well, she had no intention of lying down while he put a knife to her throat. There was no way she was making this easy for him.

Was there a back door?

The sergeant was making a call on the radio, putting out a Be On the Lookout, as he'd called it. But was it too late? Had he already gotten what he came for? Payton?

## Chapter Thirteen

Callum's fears were confirmed as he caught sight of Payton, sitting on the edge of a plastic chair in the lobby of the police substation.

"I was tricked," she said to him as he crossed the lobby. She immediately stood up to greet him, and he brought her into an embrace. Holding tight, he felt her trembling despite the determination in her eyes.

"You changed your cell phone number, right?" he asked.

"It's one of the first things I did," she admitted.

"Who has the new number?" he asked.

"Besides the police?" she asked. "No one—well, hold on. There are two places that have my new number. My old employer and my school."

"That narrows the field," he said, trying to offer some reassurance that progress could now be made.

She nodded.

"This will give the police something to work with," he continued.

"My name is Sergeant Leonard," an officer said as he approached. He offered a handshake before taking a seat opposite Payton. He scooted the orange plastic chair over toward her, to the point their knees almost knocked. His cell phone was out.

Atlas started a low, throaty growl. Callum excused them and walked him to the other side of the room. They were still within listening distance, and Atlas's wary gaze never left the sergeant.

"Did you see anything out of the ordinary on your way inside the building?" the sergeant asked.

"No, sir," she said.

"Please, call me Leo," the sergeant said in a move that surprised Callum. The older gentleman's demeanor softened. "We want this perp behind bars almost as much as I'm certain you do."

She gave a slight nod. Her moment of hesitation and closed-off demeanor said it would be impossible for them to want the man locked up more than her. A wall had come up between her and the world. One that was most likely a necessary evil for her to protect herself. Callum understood her need for self-preservation. He wished she believed she had someone else to lean on. He'd seen the same look in her eyes when they'd first met, and it nearly cracked his heart in half for the look to surface again after the two of them had become close. Back to square one. Or maybe he'd fooled himself into thinking they'd ever left in the first place.

Payton gave Leo a quick rundown of what had happened. Her gaze unfocused like she was looking inside herself when she spoke, and her voice was even, almost trancelike. Hearing the account again, this time with even more details, sent white-hot anger shooting through Callum. Was that bastard around here somewhere? Watching? He could have been keeping an eye on the parking lot, looking out for her vehicle. At least Callum had convinced her to let him drive her and Atlas to Austin. The perp might have been waiting somewhere, ready to run her off the road and finish the job. Having a witness who might be able to identify him at least partially wasn't something a career criminal could afford to have.

Callum considered their options as he listened to Payton. The perp might have seen her in Callum's vehicle. Since his truck was registered to his business in Houston and he came from a wealthy family, someone could connect the dots. Driving back should be safe as long as he made sure they weren't followed. He could use his truck or leave it here and have one of his drivers pick it up. In fact, he could have one of his drivers trade with him. That way, he could take Payton through a back door and into a new vehicle.

So, the question of how the perp managed to get Payton's new number took center stage. Could the man be some kind of tech guru?

Callum's mind shifted to wondering if the detective in charge of the case had found any links among the victims, or any commonalities. Hair color? Location? Student status? Would they share details about the case? Payton deserved to know.

He searched his memory bank to remember what the three components for a crime like murder were and came up with them: means, motive and opportunity. Motive seemed to be important to this case. What was the reason this guy killed? What was the purpose? What did he get out of it? Callum knew from an association with a Houston police officer years ago that murders weren't random. At least, not usually. They might appear to be on the surface, but Rodney Boyer had explained that once the layers were peeled back, there was always a reason. The more twisted and calculated the crimes, the more deep-seated the reason, Rodney had said. The two had struck up a friendship after sitting next to each other on Friday nights at a pub down the street from Callum's office.

Rodney had stopped by the pub after work because his wife had taken their kids to visit her folks. It gave him the chance to destress before early-morning Saturday sports, which he handled so his stay-at-home wife could sleep in. Rodney made marriage and compromise seem so easy back then. He'd been clear that parenting wasn't for the faint of heart. Any time he talked about his kids, though, he got the cheesiest smile on his face. It was easy to see how much Rodney loved his pair of boys. It had also given Callum some hope that all dads weren't as stubborn as his had been. Callum could dig his heels in when he wanted to, and he attributed the trait all the way back to his grandfather. Three generations of Hayes men with the same attribute didn't inspire a whole lot of confidence. At least his father, Logan Hayes, wasn't mean on top of it.

Their last conversation shouldn't have been the last

time they spoke. Words were said that could never be taken back. Their relationship had always been strained. With no chance to make amends, Callum would live with guilt the rest of his life.

He shifted his thoughts back to motive as he said comforting words to Atlas. The animal didn't seem too fond of the sergeant being so close to Payton. Without the medication to keep Atlas calm, this would most likely be a whole different scenario. One that would have them both outside.

"It's okay," he soothed.

Atlas's hackles raised, but Callum didn't take offense. He liked the fact Atlas was so protective of Payton. She would need the animal after Callum went back to Houston. The thought of leaving her sat like a hot poker in his gut. He needed to get used to the feeling, because Payton had made clear she would never let anyone in for long.

A couple of deep breaths later, he was able to set those heavy thoughts aside as he listened to the conversation between Payton and the sergeant.

The Masked Monster might have been turned down by a beautiful woman. Payton was beautiful. He liked to stalk them first. Was he a hunter? The connection didn't resonate. It was possible he'd grown up hunting or had a father who did.

Callum used the search engine on his phone to see what had been written about the Masked Monster so far. There'd been four victims. All four lived in apartments—not exactly a surprise, considering this was Austin. One of his victims was a waitress who worked at a popular national restaurant chain known for their burgers. Her name was Heidi. Then there was nurse Shelia. She'd worked the night shift. Another one of his victims was Rochelle, who worked in a hotel. Avery had worked at Cracker Barrel on the highway leading to the small town of Buddha, south of Austin.

The first attack had happened eleven months ago. Five attempts in less than a year was a lot. The date of the first murder didn't ring any bells. It might be significant for the perp, though. Callum wished he had Rodney's number so he could pick his brain. His experience would come in handy. As it was, Callum was basically grabbing on to anything he could remember from the bits and pieces of their last conversations before Rodney got a promotion and was moved to a different shift.

Callum looked up the reasons behind crimes on Google. He'd already guessed motive. It was an important component. Now, means and opportunity. This bastard killed women in their own homes after raping them. According to the articles, he spent roughly two hours doing what he wanted to them while making them believe if they complied he would let them live. All the while, he knew that was a lie. He was twisted, so the reasons behind his actions had to have been deep-seated. He was on a power trip with these women. The word *monster* was deceiving in some ways—he'd charmed his way into Payton's apartment under the guise of being helpful. There was no reason to believe he hadn't done something similar with the others. He also wore a mask, which wouldn't have been as easy to pull off with the other murders since the first was long before Halloween. Could he be trying to say that he had two faces?

He didn't want to be recognized as he approached the women, which made Callum believe he might be known to them. In Austin, faces blended together. There were always so many young adults on the streets in and around the capital, thanks to the large public university. It was one reason he'd picked Houston to start his business. Traffic in Austin was a nightmare at all times, and the sheer number of freshmen through seniors gave the downtown area an ant farm feel.

The perp had an ego and thought he was smarter than everyone else. He would have to in order to talk to his victims, knowing full well what he was about to do to them. He watched their coming and going habits. He stalked them for...

Callum checked the dates of the murders. They occurred between six to eight weeks apart. Would he have taken something from the others in order to relive the experience? Rodney had said something about that once. They'd discussed movies, too, and he would say what the director had gotten right versus what would have never happened. No surprise that Hollywood took a lot of liberties. The first being cases could take months, even years to solve in the real world. Getting warrants took time, unlike in the TV shows, where everything wrapped up in an hour or less.

Atlas growled. Callum looked up to see what was happening. Payton and the sergeant were standing, shaking hands.

"Thank you for the information, ma'am," the sergeant said. "We put out a BOLO and will contact you if anything changes in the case."

"How will I know it's you guys?" she asked.

"Call me to confirm," he said, handing her a business card from his pocket.

"When will you have the trace on my line?" she asked.

"That won't take long," he said. "We have tech working on it now."

"If he didn't leave DNA evidence in my home, what makes you think you'll be able to trace the call?" she asked.

"We'll do everything in our power to track this perp down," he said by way of excuse. She'd clearly touched on a question that he didn't want to answer. Because she was right.

Payton nodded, looking resigned that this nightmare wouldn't end anytime soon. Her gaze shifted to Callum, and he could have sworn he saw a split second of relief wash over her.

"Any chance we can exit through the back?" she asked.

"There's a side door if your friend wants to pull his vehicle around," he said.

Callum fished out his key fob. "Point me in a direction."

The sergeant nodded toward the east side of the building. "It's the door officers use. I'll have someone walk out with you to be sure no one is out there or tries to make a move."

As reassuring as that statement should be, the sergeant was also saying there was little they could do to protect her while this perp was on the loose. One look at Payton said she knew it, too.

But this guy didn't know whom he was dealing with, because the determined set to her chin said he would never get what he wanted from her.

## Chapter Fourteen

Payton waited with the female officer as Callum pulled the truck around. Neither spoke, and the quiet gave her time to think. Should she stick around in Austin and let him come at her again? Or retreat to the farmhouse? It only seemed like a matter of time before he found her there. Atlas was hurt and wouldn't be at full speed for weeks. If anything, she needed to protect him rather than the other way around.

She weighed her options as she thought about staying at the ranch again. Would she be putting Callum's mother and grandmother at risk? At this point, she had no idea how far this guy would go in order to get to her.

But she would be ready.

The truck pulled around, and the officer glanced over at Payton for confirmation. She nodded.

"I'll walk beside you," the officer said. She was all of five feet two inches, with her auburn hair tied back in a ponytail. "I overheard on the radio what was going on."

Payton nodded.

"I hope they catch him," she said in an attempt at solidarity.

"I do, too," Payton agreed. "But I have no plans to live my life in fear until they do."

"Good," the officer said. "Just watch your back, and don't let him sneak up on you again."

"He lost the power of surprise this time," Payton said. "I'll know he's coming next time."

The officer gave a look of solidarity before pushing open the door, taking a step out and surveying the area. She motioned for Payton to follow before walking her to the passenger door, which faced them.

"Stay safe," the officer said as Payton climbed inside the cab.

"You, too," Payton said before closing the door.

"He targets people in service jobs," Callum said the minute the officer was out of sight.

"How so?" Payton asked, wondering how he'd come up with that information.

"It's in the news stories," he said. "I'm guessing you had no interest in reading them."

"I did want to. My brain went in survival mode, and I couldn't bring myself to go back and look at the lost lives," she admitted. "I told myself that it would get easier in a few weeks and that I just needed to disappear and keep my head down."

It was time to study the details, though.

"He got ahold of your cell number. Can he get your new address from the same source he used the first time?" Callum asked. The question was legitimate.

"No, because I didn't update my address. I went

to the post office and filled out the form requesting they hold my mail. I said that I would be away from home for a few weeks," she said, realizing the move was smarter than she'd realized at the time. She'd had no idea whether or not the farmhouse would be livable, so she didn't want to make it her permanent address just yet. "I thought I'd change my address when I went back to clean out my apartment. After the attack, I just went into panic mode."

"You did better than most people would after a horrific event like the one you experienced," Callum said. "You're not giving yourself enough credit."

"I'm grateful to be alive," she said. "And I'm ready to help put this bastard behind bars. Obviously, he hasn't given up on killing me. How long before he moves on to someone else to satisfy the urge to kill again?"

Her cell phone buzzed, indicating a call was coming in before she could mention her frustration about not recognizing his voice on the phone earlier. Her pulse kicked up a couple of notches until she recognized the number as belonging to the desk sergeant.

"I wanted to pass along the information from tech. We didn't get him. He used a VPN, which basically means we can track that there was a call, just not find his location. All she could see was that data was moving around," he informed her after perfunctory greetings.

"So, what you're saying is that she could verify that a call came in when I said it did, but there is no way to figure out the location of the caller," she said, just to clarify she'd heard right the first time. The news was disappointing.

"That's correct," he confirmed.

"Should I change this number and not tell anyone but you guys?" she asked.

"That is up to your discretion," he said. She picked up on a tone in his voice that she couldn't quite put a finger on.

"Is there a benefit in keeping this number where he can call and harass me?" she asked.

"We might be able to pick up clues in the background noise as to his location if you called the number," he said. "Or he might speak, slip up and give something away."

"I could ask him to meet me and then not show up," she hedged, almost immediately realizing he would be smarter than that. Still, it was something.

"True," he said with hesitation in his voice. He had to be thinking along the same lines. "This goes without saying, but we would like for you to stay as far away from him as possible for your own safety."

"Believe me, I intend to do just that," she said. "Besides, baiting him into a trap would only backfire. He seems to be thinking one step ahead of me."

"He has more experience in this than you do," the sergeant pointed out. She couldn't argue there.

"Thank you for the update," she said when there was nothing left to say. The Masked Monster was on a hunt to kill her. She had no plans to let him. Right now, they were at a stalemate.

"Detective Lansing will contact you if anything

else comes up," the sergeant said. "You might want to program both his and my number into your cell so it won't show up as an unknown caller."

"Will do," she said before ending the call. She turned to Callum. "I'm sure you picked up the gist of the conversation."

"I did," he confirmed.

"Should we stop and give Atlas water?" she asked, figuring there wasn't much else to say about the perp right now.

"He took down almost a whole bottle while you were inside the station," he said.

She nodded as she looked out the windshield.

"Are you getting hungry?" he asked.

"I was before all this happened," she said on a sigh. "But I should probably eat something."

"With Atlas, I'd rather not try to eat inside anywhere," he said. "There's fast food on the next couple of exits."

"I could probably eat a burger and French fries," she said. "A Coke would be nice. My morning caffeine has already worn off, and I can feel a whopper of a headache coming on."

"Stress and hunger can do that," he agreed.

"So, we're down to someone getting my records from school, my former employer or the cops," she said, circling back to the earlier conversation.

"I hope we can rule out law enforcement," he stated. "People sworn to protect shouldn't be predators."

"Agreed," she said. "Which leaves my school files

or my work. Do you think it's possible this guy works on campus somewhere? That would give him access to the computer system."

"He might. Should we turn around and head to UT?" he asked.

"It's a thought," she said. "Although all I keep thinking is how much I want to get out of Austin and as far away from him as possible."

"No one could blame you," he stated. "We could pick up a burner phone and you could call all the departments you interact with at school. Since you know the sound of his voice and he won't be expecting the call to be you, we might be able to catch him off guard."

"That's a good point. Other than blue eyes and an average build, I have no other way to know if I'm walking right past him when I'm crossing campus," she said with another shiver. "The thought gives me the willies."

"Since he knows what you look like, that would put us at a disadvantage," he observed.

"Which is the last thing we want," she said. "I already feel like I'm grasping at straws here."

"Since his victims all work in service jobs, they might have crossed paths during work hours," he stated.

"What kinds of jobs?" she asked.

"A student, a hotel lobby employee, two waitresses and a nurse," he said. "He could have been slighted by an employer or a female boss."

"That would explain the killings. What about the

rape aspect?" she asked as an involuntary shiver rocked her body. Every time she thought of what might have happened, her imagination started running wild. In this case, she couldn't fathom the horrors of what this man did to his victims.

"Good question," he said.

"He was polite. It's how he convinced me to let him inside my apartment. He was pretending to be helpful," she said out loud.

"His manners were purely meant to manipulate," he said. "Sounds like he had an overbearing person in his life. Someone female."

"And now he wants revenge," she finished for him. "Someone he wants to abuse and then punish."

"He might have sexual abuse in his background," he offered. "Someone who was supposed to care for him abused him physically, sexually, emotionally."

"You want to feel sorry for someone like that until you know what he does to others," she said. "This guy we're talking about. Wouldn't he live close to his victims?"

"Considering they're all in Austin, I'd say the answer is yes," he said. "Keep in mind that I have no law enforcement training. I did, however, have a buddy once who was on the force. He used to tell me stories."

"You don't still happen to be friends with this guy, do you?" she asked.

"I haven't seen him in a while at the bar," he stated as he navigated off the highway. "The only thing he ever told me was how rare it was for someone in law enforcement to commit a crime. He hated all those movies that gave cops a bad name. But the bad seeds are the worst kind."

She nodded.

"I can see that," she said. "They already know how an investigation is going to go, what steps would be taken and potentially who would be assigned to the investigation."

"And they know how to keep their own DNA out of a crime scene," he pointed out.

"Just like in my case," she stated. "I don't remember any cops coming into the coffee shop who would come close to fitting the description of this guy."

"Who else would know how to keep DNA out of a crime scene?" he asked.

"Someone who works in a hospital, like a doctor," she said. They were both thinking out loud at this point. It was good to have someone to bounce ideas off and even better that she could finally talk to someone about what had happened.

"Or anyone who works in a lab," he said.

"I could see that," she said. "Do we have locations of the other victims? Did they write about where the crimes occurred?"

"We can pull over and map it out," he said.

"Since we're already on the way home, let's stick with our plan to grab a bite and eat on the road. Atlas will need dinner by the time we get home, and we don't have any provisions with us," she said. This was the second time recently she felt unprepared. The perp was one step ahead of them, and they were always playing catch-up. They needed to flip it and figure out his next move so they could head him off. The police were doing everything they could to locate him, but since he was still walking around scot-free, she couldn't depend on them entirely. "We can map everything out tonight when my head is clear and I can think straight."

The last thing she wanted to do was run off half-cocked and play right into his hands.

"Okay," he said. "We can make a map of the victims' homes but also their workplaces to see if we can find any patterns or similarities."

This felt like the right path. The police would be doing the same thing, but she and Callum would be looking at this through a different lens. That might help with the investigation. Besides, she couldn't hide any longer, since he seemed to have resources to find her. The advantage was all on his side, considering he knew exactly what she looked like.

It would be nice if there was something else about him that stuck out. He'd been able to hide his face with the *Beauty and the Beast* mask and his build with the costume. Halloween had already happened, so there wouldn't be a reason for him to be out and about in his getup.

"After we map out the locations, what do you think about heading back to Austin in the morning to stop off at the victims' workplaces?" he asked. "Who knows what information we might get from coworkers or bosses?"

"It can't hurt," she said. Then again, they might be walking right into his backyard.

"I'll see if my mother and Granny would be okay watching Atlas," he said. "He doesn't seem to mind them, and he might not be up for another trip."

"He would probably do better with a day of rest and I can't imagine him being with better people," she agreed.

Callum's smile sent warmth through her.

"I'll be able to let you take the lead with talking to people," he said. "I can hang back and we can pretend not to know each other."

"It would give you a chance to see if anyone around was acting suspicious," she continued for him.

"That's what I'm hoping," he said. "Since this guy spent time watching you, he probably knows that you're single. I'm guessing he only targets single women with no one to get in his way."

"I know the detective on the case isn't flowing information this way, and I guess I understand his need to keep quiet," she said. "If we study the other cases, we might get some clues into his personality, which could give us an advantage."

"If we find him at his workplace or where he lives, I'm certain that we'll see some kind of reaction," he said.

Yes, but what they were planning to do was the equivalent of walking into the jaws of a lion. And they had no idea how the perp would react. No matter how awful the thought of coming face-to-face with him again might be, there was no other choice.

## Chapter Fifteen

Callum gave their order before snaking around to the pickup and pay window. He'd never been big on fast food, mainly due to the portion size. This would be more of a snack for him than anything else, but it would keep his stomach from growling on the way home. Plus, Payton needed food now. Her headache was no doubt a combination of hunger and stress. Lack of caffeine probably didn't help.

He pulled around, settled up and was handed a bag along with two drinks and straws. The worker tried to hand over everything all at once. He did his level best to keep up, shifting items over to Payton as fast as he could.

The parking lot was a good place to park for a few minutes, long enough for him to polish off his meal so he could get back on the highway. Folks who tried to drive and eat weren't helping with Texas's reputation for dangerous highways, and it didn't take long to gobble down the fast food.

"I didn't realize how hungry I was," Payton said

as she munched on a fry. "You were right about food helping with my head."

"Good." Callum wanted to ease some of her burden.

"It's so easy to get busy and forget to eat," she stated.

"Sounds like you have too much on your plate if you don't have time for the basics," he said, even though he understood. He probably wasn't much better in the early days of starting his business.

"Having school and a job is not for the faint of heart," she said. "I'm not exactly a morning person, either."

"That can't help when you're opening a coffee shop at…what?…6:00 a.m.?" he asked.

"Five," she corrected.

"Not even the chickens get up that early," he joked, hoping to lighten some of the tension.

"My mind keeps going back to that phone call," she said, circling back to their earlier conversation. "Why didn't I recognize his voice?"

"He might have gotten someone else to make the call for him," he offered. "The person could have believed it was a prank call."

She nodded before chewing on another fry. She fed one to Atlas, who perked up at the smell. He snatched the fry and swallowed so fast there was no way he chewed it.

"Did he even taste it?" she asked with a small smile.

"The smell must be satisfying enough for him.

That and the bite," he said. "Because he most certainly couldn't have tasted it."

Payton shook her head.

"What if I'm remembering his voice wrong?" she asked. "This whole ordeal has me questioning myself."

"Your brain may have blocked out some details in order to protect you," he said. "The voice has been the one thing you've been clear on."

"I thought so, too," she said. "What if I'm wrong?"

"Then, that's okay, too," he said. "Last night was the first good night of sleep you've had in a little more than a week. You're trying to recover from something that had to be the scariest moments of your life. It's okay if you remember something wrong or second-guess yourself right now. I believe you'll know if you hear him again. Plus, law enforcement will dot every i and cross every t before they make an arrest. All you're trying to do if figure out who this perp might be. They'll do the rest."

"You're right," she said. She was being too hard on herself because she didn't want to give this perp the chance to strike again. "At least I won't be hiding any longer."

"No. You won't," he reassured. "And I'll be right there, watching your back, making sure nothing bad happens. You're not alone any longer."

She blinked a couple of times, like she was blinking back tears.

"You have no idea how much that means to me," she said. "And Atlas, too. We both need you."

Payton couldn't even guess how his heart warmed at those words. She deserved to have a person in her life who looked out for her for a change. She should be surrounded by people who loved her. There wasn't a mean bone in her body. She was compassionate and kind. She should have the world in her palm, not be forced to struggle or hide from a sicko. She was everything that was right in the world, and she deserved a hand up, especially considering the fact she would never ask for one. As it was, she was working to put herself through school. He'd had to work at getting her to allow him to help. He had a feeling she would go out of her way to do the same for others.

They had a plan now—a plan that had to work so she could put this behind her and move on with her life. He couldn't see a way to do that if she had to constantly look over her shoulder or worry someone might jump out from behind a piece of furniture or an opened door.

And, selfishly, he couldn't imagine her being able to truly let him while she had to worry about her life being taken at any moment. No one knew how much time they had on this earth. His grandfather's untimely death from heat exhaustion was all the reminder Callum needed of the fact.

There were two guarantees: life would be short and unpredictable. Even someone who was considered to have lived a long time only saw about ninety first days of spring. Callum had been thinking a lot about death since losing his grandfather. He'd been thinking about how much time was wasted on trivial arguments. He couldn't even remember what they'd been arguing about the last time they'd had words—words that made him feel like a class-A jerk now that his grandfather was gone.

If Callum had said the sky was blue, Duncan would have argued it was green. If Callum had said lilies were white, Duncan would have contradicted with purple. If Callum had said summers in Texas were hot, Duncan would have put on a sweater to prove they were cold.

Callum wished for one more day with his grandfather, if only to ask him why. Would it really have been so hard to agree for once? Not that Callum hadn't learned to dig in his heels. He was just as much to blame and egged on his grandfather at every turn.

Maybe he should ask himself why.

Then, there was his mother's request for the family to come home. She looked strong, so he didn't think it had anything to do with her physical condition. Although there were illnesses that looked fine on the surface. He'd cornered her about a medical diagnosis when she'd first called, and she'd promised her health was good. Her mind seemed sound, too.

Though he could admit to ducking out the first chance he got yesterday morning to take muffins over to Payton. Granted, he'd been cornered in the kitchen and his mother had made it clear she wasn't divulging any details until the others arrived.

The thought of all six Hayes siblings being home at one time had its appeal. But the others had been clear they wouldn't be coming. Callum was supposed to find a way to break the news to his mother. Of course, seeing her and Granny living alone on the ranch did cause more than a twinge of guilt to hit him.

There were ranch hands and a foreman, so it wasn't like they were completely alone. And yet, it seemed wrong for the two of them to sit alone at the big table every night for supper when Callum remembered how lively dinners had been with his brothers and sisters home.

Duncan might have ruled with an iron fist, but he seemed able to relax for a little while at dinners. Why did Callum so easily recall all the bad times with his grandfather and so easily forget the good?

Damn. The realization smacked him in the face as he looked out at the long stretch of highway in front of him. How much of a jerk did it make him that he focused on the painful memories when there were good ones, too?

A huge one.

Were his brothers and sisters doing the same? Was there anything Callum could do to help them realize it if they were?

He set those heavy thoughts aside, promising to do better while he was home. He still wasn't ready to drop the life he'd built in Houston, but he could be a whole lot better about visiting more often. Granny might be spry, but she was getting up there in years. Who knew how many Christmases she had left?

Didn't that notion cause the fast food in his stomach to churn? He'd missed a whole lot of years with her over his feud with his grandfather. How silly did all that seem now?

More than he wanted to admit. While he was on the road, maybe he should give his brothers and sisters a call and tell each one that it might be a good idea to come home after all. It might not make a difference to anyone but him that he'd made the attempt. How much worse would he feel if they lost Granny or his mother without trying to get his siblings home?

A whole lot.

Glancing over at Payton, he noticed that she was sleeping. Since he didn't want to wake her, he decided to hold off on those phone calls for the time being. He could call his siblings tonight once he and Payton had gone over their plan.

"WE'RE HOME" came the familiar voice—a voice that soothed Payton. A gentle shake caused her to stir and her eyes to open. Callum stood outside the door on the passenger side of the vehicle, leaning toward her, with his hand on her knee. Contact caused warmth to pulse up her leg to parts she didn't want to think about right now while she was trying to wake up.

Payton blinked a couple of times, trying to shake the fog.

"I fell asleep?" she asked, realizing she was beginning to make a habit of that in his presence.

"Only for a couple of hours," he said, standing beside her with a small smile. Did he realize how gorgeous he was when he did that? The smile was barely a dry crack in his lips and still made him even sexier.

She shouldn't be too surprised. The man was sex-in-a-bucket hot. Getting to know his personality only made him that much more attractive.

It was almost easy to forget she was running for her life when she looked into those honest eyes of his. Almost.

She yawned and stretched before taking the hand being held out to help her out of the passenger seat. Her legs had gone numb and her knees decided to buckle. His strong hands were around her, steadying her before she had time to react.

"Sorry for being bad company on the road," she said after thanking him for keeping her upright. She balanced against the truck as she shook life back into her legs one at a time.

"No problem," he said as she regained her footing. The blood came back to her limbs, and she could trust them to hold her steady on their own.

"I fell asleep thinking about who he could possibly be," she said.

"Did you come up with any ideas?" He perked up, and she figured he'd churned over ideas as much as she had on the ride home.

"Theories mostly," she clarified. "This person operates on the fringes of our circles."

He nodded agreement as she stepped aside to allow him access to Atlas.

"He isn't someone I know or interact with on a regular basis. Me and the others," she added.

"I thought about that, too," Callum admitted after helping Atlas down. The dog jogged off and then did his business. The couple hours' round trip was a lot of sitting still in one day, so she figured taking a walk would do them both some good. "And I agree, by the way."

"It makes sense, right?" she asked but it was more statement than question. "That he is someone we know but don't have a lot of one-on-one interaction with. Otherwise, he would stand out in my mind. I would have noticed him being nervous or I would have picked up on something awkward about him."

"Anyone can be charming for a couple of minutes," he seemed to agree. "This is someone on the periphery of your life back in Austin."

"I think it might be helpful if we could speak to the victims' friends and coworkers. See what information we can glean from them. Then, we circle any touch points that cross over. I keep thinking there has to be some common ground in our lives," she said.

"We already know his victims worked in the service industry. A nurse is someone who helps others. Although not directly a service job," he surmised. "And we know there's at least one other student."

"Did you mention whether or not she had a part-time job?" she asked.

"There was nothing in the article," he said.

"We have names, so we can check social media accounts to figure out who their closest friends were," she said. "They would most likely be the ones who commented the most, and we would be able to identify them based on their pictures."

Payton had never been a fan of putting her life

out for everyone to see on social media. Plus, she didn't have a whole lot of free time. Her mother followed her online, too. Payton figured if her mother wanted to know about her life, she could pick up a phone and call.

"That will help with the student," he said, walking beside her as Atlas led the way.

The sun was already descending, and the sky out here on the ranch was vast and incredible. It seemed to go on forever. Purple and orange hues painted the heavens. The colors swirled together and twisted around as the bright yellow orb kissed the treetops.

This was the reason she lived in Texas—the landscape and the sense of space. She felt like she could breathe here, and no one had a right to take that away from her.

# Chapter Sixteen

Callum was anxious to make headway on Payton's case. And yet, he didn't want this peaceful moment to end. She stopped and stared at a sunset that could only be described as Mother Nature showing off. The beautiful skies tugged at his heartstrings and made him question why he would let a fight with his grandfather force him out of town.

He would have argued until the cows came home that he didn't leave at eighteen because of Duncan Hayes. Life had taken over, and he hadn't stopped once to consider his reasonings after he left town and never looked back. Now, his regrets kept playing on repeat.

Callum wasn't the only one to blame. His grandfather had made it impossible to stay. The fact that all six Hayes grandkids left the ranch the minute they'd turned eighteen spoke for itself. Still, placing all the blame on his grandfather didn't seem right. Just like accusing Hannah of being solely responsible for the demise of their relationship wouldn't be fair. Part of being a grown-up meant taking responsibility for his wrongs. Right off the bat, he could see that communication wasn't his strong suit. Work had forced him to be a better communicator or else lose all of his employees. He'd developed the skill set there. Why was it so much harder to apply those same lessons in his personal life?

Setting those thoughts aside for now, he refocused. Atlas was walking better. Being gored by a wild hog was no joke. Callum had taken a tusk to the calf once as he climbed a tree while trying to get out of its way. Stitches were no fun. Though he'd had more than his fair share growing up wild as a buck on this land.

A whole mess of good memories flooded him. Like the time he and Rory stayed out on the tire swing pushing each other until the darn thing broke. Rory had broken his left arm in the fall from the swing they'd nicknamed Grace. For years after all of the siblings teased Rory about his fall from Grace. The inside joke had followed him through high school.

Then, there was Callum's first kiss around the back side of the barn. He'd fallen head over heels for Angela Hawkins, the most popular girl in school. The term *opposites attract* had applied to their short-lived relationship. Turned out, she only got close to Callum so she could flirt with Rory.

Callum had expected a whole lot of teasing for falling for that one, but his siblings only gave each other a hard time about surface stuff. Broken hearts had been off-limits. Rory, of course, had refused to go out with her. Someone started a rumor that she had bad breath, and Callum was pretty certain it came from one of his younger brothers, though no one ever stepped up to claim rights to it.

Angela had survived the rumor just fine. Like most of its kind, it died down in a matter of weeks and she was behind the bleachers kissing Cordis Wheeler not a month later. Callum had started to apologize to her after he realized one of his brothers was behind the whole mess, but she flipped him off the minute she saw him walking across the cafeteria toward her. He changed course and took a pass on feeling sorry for her.

Countless games of tag and capture the flag had been played on these grounds. There'd been cookouts and barbecues out here. Why were those so easy to forget and the bad memories so quick to take their place?

Payton touched his arm and nodded toward Atlas, who seemed to have locked onto something in the tree line. The shift in focus yanked him out of his reverie. It wasn't likely that hogs were this close to the main house and barns, considering all the traffic at the ranch. The bunkhouse was behind the barns, and hands came and went throughout the day. Callum had yet to go say hello to Deacon Wade. He went back a long way with Callum's grandfather and the details of how the two met and got to know each other were still fuzzy. Either Callum didn't remember them or they'd gone to great lengths to cover them up.

Deacon wasn't even Mr. Wade's first name, that much Callum knew. He got the name because his daddy was a preacher in a small town near Corpus Christi. Deacon had taken the opposite route, and Callum had overheard his mother coming to Deacon's defense. She'd said his criminal record was from a long time ago, when he was a different man, and should be left there. She'd argued a person's past didn't always determine their future and that forgiveness was important to people who claimed to be Christians. His mother knew how to throw up an argument.

Speaking of Deacon, there were plenty of ranching families who turned over the business to a ranch manager when none of the siblings wanted to take over the responsibilities. Callum should suggest doing that with Deacon. No one knew Hayes Cattle like their current foreman.

Atlas took a couple of tentative steps toward the tree line. Half of his legs were hidden by scrub brush, but the visible half of his body showed signs of being on full alert. Ears tuned toward the noise and hackles raised, he was making slow and methodical progress toward whatever he was fixated on.

This wasn't a good sign. Part of Callum wanted to ask Payton to stay put while he investigated. Doing so didn't ensure her safety. A good shooter could take her out while she stood in the open and then disappear into the trees before anyone had a chance to react.

Callum reached for Payton's hand and then clasped their fingers. To an outsider, they looked like a couple. All he could think about right now was finding a way to keep her and Atlas safe.

He had promised to keep Payton's secret when danger stayed across the street. If his family was going to be threatened, there needed to be a meeting.

His mother and Granny needed to know what they faced, as well as Deacon and the rest of the hands. Any one of them could be caught unaware, and Callum wouldn't put their lives in danger unnecessarily.

"You're okay," Callum soothed as they reached Atlas. He glanced at Payton before saying, "Stay low and stick with him while I check and see what's out there."

She started to argue but then snapped her mouth shut. She seemed to realize Atlas could go off at any minute, and he listened to her the best. She gave a quick nod of approval.

Callum didn't wait for her to change her mind. Instead, he crouched as low as possible and made his way toward whatever had caught Atlas's attention. He reminded himself it could be nothing. No one had followed them home. He'd made certain by checking the rearview mirror repeatedly on the drive.

It occurred to him the perp might have caught sight of Callum's license plate, but that would direct the bastard to Houston, not the ranch. Even so, with a famous, wealthy last name like his, connections could be made. Still, the probability he was here was slim to none. Anything could have set off Atlas. This could be a rabbit, for all Callum knew. To be safe, Callum would treat this as a real threat.

He breached the tree line and heard the sound of twigs snapping to his left. Chasing this down would require him to go deeper inside the trees, leaving Payton exposed. Since she had Atlas, Callum could risk it.

Tracking the sound, he looked for signs of a human.

He would like to be able to pick up on a footprint, but light was running out, and he couldn't risk using his flashlight. Since he could no longer see the yard, he decided to double back.

As Callum turned, a twig snapped to his right. He moved behind a tree trunk and waited. Exactly five seconds later, a figure came into view. It was too dark at this point to make out the form clearly.

He held his breath, waiting for the person to get close enough for him to tackle from behind once they passed by him. Patience won battles, and he'd learned a long time ago that stillness came in a close second.

The figure moved near his tree trunk. The breeze carried a familiar scent, and he knew exactly who it was.

"Mother," he said.

She gasped.

"Callum, is that you?" she asked.

"Yes," he said, standing up and turning on the flashlight app on his cell phone so he could see her. "What are you doing out here?"

"The same thing you are," she said as she got close enough for him to make out her features. A shotgun was tucked underneath her right arm.

He doubted it.

MUCH TO PAYTON'S SURPRISE, Callum came walking out of the woods with his mother at his side. Furthermore, Marla had a shotgun. Atlas seemed to recognize them both even from a distance. His ears relaxed, and he trotted toward them.

"Everything okay out there?" Payton asked as she met them halfway. It was almost completely dark at this point.

"Whoever was out there is gone now," Marla stated. "We should go inside and talk."

"Does this have something to do with the reason you wanted to call everyone home?" Callum asked.

"It might," his mother said. "I'd hoped to lay my cards on the table once everyone was here. Since you've kept one eye on the door since arriving yesterday, I'm guessing that's not going to happen."

The trio reached the main house and slipped in the back door to the kitchen. Payton set about feeding Atlas and giving him his nighttime dose of medication. As she refilled his water bowl, Granny joined them.

"Everyone has built lives away from here," Callum said to his mother in a soft tone, like he was trying to let her down easy.

"I know why everyone left," she said. "I'm confused about the reason no one seems to want to come back now that your grandfather is gone. It feels like I did something to run everyone off."

"It's not you and never was," he said quickly. "In fact, that's probably the most unfortunate consequence of how everything ended up shaking out. Before we get into all that, who were you looking for out there?"

"There have been threats," Marla admitted. She placed the shotgun in the pantry before turning to meet Callum's gaze. "Ever since your grandfather…"

Marla couldn't seem to bring herself to say the rest of the words out loud. She shot a look toward Callum, and he nodded in acknowledgment.

"What threats?" he immediately asked.

Granny made a tsk-tsk sound, which drew Marla's ire.

"What was I supposed to do?" Marla asked. "He caught me red-handed out there trying to figure out who was slinking through my woods."

"Could be poachers," he said as he put up a hand. "I know they don't normally come so close to the main house."

"No. They don't," Marla confirmed. "It's not likely to be them."

"How are these threats being delivered?" he asked.

"Graffiti on the barn, on the main house and again on my truck. All the events have been spaced apart, so at first I believed teenagers were getting out of hand or a band of no-good folks were squatting on our land, making themselves known," she began. "Then, I got a text warning me about sticking around in Cider Creek."

"You've lived here for your entire life. Why would you move now?" Callum asked.

"That's not the right question to ask," Granny said, wagging her finger.

"And what is?" Callum asked his grandmother.

"Who wants to take this place over?" Granny asked.

"Is that why you want us to come home?" Callum turned to his mother. "For a united front?"

"That, and for a direction," Marla stated. "This

ranch was your grandfather's heart and soul before he died. Your grandfather built a legacy that sadly ended too soon. In the end, he decided it should go to you all. I know the two of you didn't see eye to eye, and you know how I felt about the way he was with all six of you."

"But?" Callum asked.

"I'm here fighting for a legacy that none of you seem to want," she continued. "We need to have a family meeting so I can lay my cards on the table with all of you in the room. Then we'll decide what to do with this place together."

"This ranch is your home," he said to her.

"Things change," she stated on a shrug. "It was your father's and my dream to take over for your grandfather one day. We always envisioned the six of you taking your rightful places and learning the family business. You've taken other paths, and I'm not here to tell any one of you that you made the wrong decision. I don't mind standing and fighting, but there's no reason to put my life on the line or anyone else's for a dream that died with your grandfather."

Callum stood there for a long moment. Granny's right hand fisted as she took a seat at the table. She seemed to be holding back what was really on her mind. Marla didn't seem to be coming all the way clean, either. She was too busy gauging Callum's responses, as though she was testing how far she should go.

Payton could see tension in the muscles in Callum's face, especially the worry lines etched in his forehead.

"I'm here now, and I'm sticking around for the

foreseeable future," he said to his mother. "I'll make sure the others know that they should come home as quickly as possible. In the meantime, I need to know who knows about the threats."

"Okay," Marla said. "Deacon for one. He met with the hands to let them know they should be more careful. Mike in security is aware there could be an additional threat."

"It's good that everyone here is in the loop," he said, and then he caught Payton's gaze. There was an additional threat lurking as long as she stayed on the ranch. Callum didn't need to point it out, since she could tell by the way he looked at her. His family deserved to know the Masked Monster might be out there somewhere. As much as Payton wanted— no, needed—to fly under the radar, it hardly seemed fair or safe to keep the information from them. Especially now that he'd found out her cell number. As much as she most likely prayed he couldn't find any other details about her, there were no promises there. He shouldn't have gotten hold of her cell.

Payton gave a slight nod, indicating her agreement. The family needed to know what they might be dealing with in addition to whatever else was happening here with the threats to the ranch.

"Anyone else want a cup of coffee?" Callum asked. "Payton and I have something to share, and I need a caffeine boost before we get into it."

Heads nodded, including Payton's. The thought of talking about what happened didn't seem to scare her as much now. He hoped it was because she felt safe with the people in the room. Or maybe it was the way they nodded, like they'd been expecting an update.

Based on the worried look in her eyes, she seemed to hope that she hadn't brought more trouble to the ranch.

## Chapter Seventeen

Callum gave his mother and Granny the short version of what had happened to Payton. Granny moved first when he was finished, pulling Payton into a hug. His mother wasn't far behind.

"I'm not sure I should stay here given the circumstances," Payton said after they reclaimed their seats around the table. "I'm afraid my being here will only add to the danger, and you guys have enough on your plate already."

"Nonsense," Granny stated without hesitation. "You belong here as much as any one of us."

"My mother is right," Marla weighed in. "We don't turn our backs on folks we care about when the going gets tough."

These were but a few of the things he missed about ranch life—how much they stuck together through thick and thin. Once someone got inside his mother's or Granny's heart, there was no going back.

"What happened to you certainly wasn't your fault," Granny continued. "What kind of people would we be to let you face that son of a—"

Granny stopped herself before finishing the sentence. She broke into a mischievous smile.

"You get my point," she said before picking up her coffee cup, pinkie out, dainty as anyone pleased and like she hadn't almost just dropped an uncharacteristic curse word.

"I heard about what happened to one of his victims while picking up the mail at the post office last week," his mother said as she shook her head. "He's sick in the head."

"And coming after me," Payton pointed out.

"Atlas makes a whole lot more sense now," Granny stated. "Seems like most young women these days prefer those purse dogs."

"And the fact that you showed up in the middle of the night one day and took up residence across the street long before it could have been ready," his mother added.

"I had to get out of Austin and remembered my great-aunt had left me her place," Payton said. "Honestly, I had no idea what to do with it at the time and still don't know how I'm going to get through all the renovations on my budget, but I won't let that stop me. I came here to temporarily escape a monster but being here makes me feel close to her again. I miss our talks even though we didn't speak to each other nearly enough."

"Beverly loved you," Granny said. "And I miss her, too."

"Did she talk about me?" Payton asked. Her eyebrow shot up in surprise.

"She did," Granny confirmed. "She was so proud of you. I hope you don't mind me saying, but she said you'd had it rough with your parents. She admired how strong you were. Said you were a go-getter, which was her highest compliment."

Granny smiled at the memory, and Callum realized she'd lost a friend when Beverly died.

"We used to have coffee together on Thursday mornings," Granny continued. "Bingo on Saturday nights until the fall, of course."

"You must have been the friend she hated leaving behind when she had to go into a home closer to me those last few months," Payton said. "I know how hard it was for her to leave Cider Creek behind. I can honestly say that I really didn't get it until I met Callum and then you two. People here look out for each other."

She glanced toward Callum, and his heart squeezed.

"That's right," Granny agreed. "Beverly would have my hide if I let you walk out that door by yourself."

"I would never allow that to happen," Callum said quickly. A little too quickly? The short answer was yes. He'd jumped the gun, and eyebrows raised. "Not while I'm here," he added. "You raised me too well for that."

He wasn't exactly sure why he added the last part except that he wasn't ready to talk about what was happening between the two of them.

"We wouldn't have done our jobs if you thought anything otherwise," Granny offered by way of accepting his bailout. He shot her a look of thanks before taking a sip of coffee.

"Payton and I are planning a trip to Austin tomorrow to track down friends and coworkers of his past victims to see if we can find any common threads," he said. "After hearing about the threats to the ranch, I'm concerned about leaving."

"A day won't make a difference one way or the other," his mother said, dismissing his concern with a wave of her hand. "Plus, I have Deacon and Mike. All the hands are aware of potential trouble. Everyone is ready to dig their heels in and fight."

"And you?" he asked. "Is that really what you want?"

"I won't be run off this property. Like you said earlier, this is my home, and no one has the right to kick me out of it," she said with her trademark defiance. She'd been described as feisty more than once. *Spirited* was another word that came to mind when thinking about his mother. Callum might have gotten his stubborn streak from his grandfather, but he got his temper from her.

"If you think you'll be all right for a day," he started.

"We'll be more than fine," his mother reassured.

"What about Atlas?" Granny asked. "Any chance you'll leave him here with us?"

"I was hoping to," he said. "If it's not too much trouble."

"Are you kidding?" Granny piped in. "It'll give me something to do besides twiddle my thumbs while

Annie Oakley over here brandishes her shotgun at every other noise."

Callum laughed at the joke, but he also realized the situation at home was more serious than his mother was trying to let on. The realization concerned him.

"You said Deacon is in the loop," Callum said to his mother.

She nodded.

"Is he fully aware of what's happening and exactly what the threats are?" he continued.

"Everyone has been told to be on watch for any unusual activity," his mother explained. "I don't have to tell you the kinds of folks Deacon has tracked over the years when there's been a threat to the livestock."

"As I recall, he was right up there with the best trackers in the county," Callum said.

"None better than the six of you," his mother corrected. "Taking the Hayeses out of the equation, then you are correct."

"No offense, but Deacon has worked this ranch for as long as I can remember, which puts him at an advanced age," he stated. "It might be time to bring in young blood." He put up a hand before his mother could argue. "Not to replace him but to offer support."

Deacon was like an uncle to Callum, and he couldn't imagine the ranch without him.

"That's what I'm trying to do," his mother stated after a long pause.

Right. She wanted her children home to take their rightful places. Callum and his siblings had other ideas about their futures. And they were right back to square one.

A question struck.

"What would happen to Deacon and the others if we decided to sell this place?" Callum asked. Based on the way his mother's face muscles tensed at the word *sell*, he figured he'd stepped on a line that he didn't want to cross.

"He'd be out of a job unless the new owners wanted to keep him on," his mother said. She was working the edge of the table with her fingers and seemed to have no idea she was doing it.

"What about hiring him to be ranch manager while we step back from the day-to-day?" Callum asked, figuring it was the best way to keep everyone's jobs. A new owner would most likely keep the current crew on until they got up and running and then get rid of them in one fell swoop. Callum couldn't allow that to happen to the good people who'd been loyal to Hayes Cattle.

He issued a sharp sigh. Deciding what to do with the ranch wasn't going to be as cut-and-dried as he'd originally believed. The notion this situation would work itself out without his intervention was so off base that it was in another ballpark. Callum resolved to call his siblings home. There was no way any one of them would want Deacon to be displaced.

"I've thought about it in order to save Deacon's job as well as the others'," his mother stated. "It's something to think about."

He knew that tone from his mother. She was trying to hide how disappointed she was that Callum and his siblings weren't running back to the ranch. To be honest, it wasn't until a little while ago when he was outside and remembering all the good times that he even had a twinge of excitement at the thought of being here.

Looking at his mother, he could tell there was something else on her mind that she wasn't saying.

"Are the threats the only thing going on?" he asked outright, figuring she might not tell him, but it didn't hurt to ask.

"Aren't those enough?" she asked, artfully dodging a real response. Her nonresponse told him everything he needed to know. There was more. His sense of urgency about reaching out to his siblings just ramped up a couple of notches. His mother was hiding something.

"For now," he said. "But we need to—"

"Is anyone else starving?" Granny asked, pushing up to standing and effectively cutting him off.

Heads nodded, and he conceded this wasn't the time to continue down this road. In his immediate future, he needed to come up with plan for tomorrow.

"THAT CHICKEN-FRIED steak with mashed potatoes and fried okra was absolute perfection," Payton said as she polished off the last bite. Funny how she hadn't thought she would be hungry after all the stress of the day, and yet here she'd cleaned her plate. The food was amazing, and the smells had had her stomach growling long before she sat down to eat.

"It was mighty good," Granny agreed. "A real treat, since I've been on a health kick lately."

"You look amazing," Payton said. "And you wouldn't let me cook, by the way. So, the least you can do is allow me to clean up."

"Nonsense," Granny said, waving her off as Callum started clearing the table.

"Let me make coffee, then," she said, biting back a yawn. She shook it off. "I've slept more in the last twenty-four hours than a whole week combined, so I have no idea why I'm still so tired."

"Being tired can catch up to you," Granny said before adding, "and I'd love a cup."

"Coming right up," Payton said. Callum practically beamed as she walked past him. She made a mental note to ask him later why her making coffee seemed to put him in a better mood. The tension and stress of finding out his mother had been threatened looked to be weighing heavily on him since hearing the news. It was understandable.

From what she gathered so far, Callum had come home to get the lay of the land for him and his siblings.

Payton turned over the ideas as she put on a pot of coffee. As she pulled cups from the cabinet while Callum rinsed plates and his mother loaded the dishwasher, it struck her that this was as close to a family moment as she'd had in her life. Suddenly, the world righted itself, and she felt like she was exactly where she wanted and needed to be.

It wouldn't last. It couldn't last. But she wouldn't

let that freeze the warmth wrapping around her at the idea of truly being part of a family.

A surprising tear slid down her cheek. She turned her face away from the two of them and secretly wiped at the trail. She could only hope Granny hadn't picked up on the move. She was quick and had a sharp mind. Time might have slowed her down physically but took away nothing mentally.

Payton filled four cups before walking them over to the table in pairs of twos. She refilled Atlas's bowl and then let him outside, walking next to him while he found a good spot to do his business. She walked back inside to a quiet and peaceful room.

Locking the door behind her, she rejoined the others at the table.

"We should probably start planning for tomorrow," Callum said to her. A sense of dread filled her at the thought of going through the details of four dead women's lives. They would have to poke around on social media pages and read the news articles.

She nodded despite the fact her stomach threatened to revolt.

"I can look through all the details if you want to be the note keeper," Callum offered after locking gazes with her. He seemed to pick up on her hesitation. "You could pull up Google Maps and figure out the most efficient way to go about this once we get addresses."

"I'm good at organizing things," she agreed, thankful for the reprieve. She would have to look at the faces of the victims on their social media pages. She needed to know what they looked like, and she hoped they could find a connection among all five of them, some kind of common thread. The thought of mapping out the spots where the home invasions occurred caused an icy chill to race down her spine.

She took in a fortifying breath.

"I'll just be upstairs reading if anyone needs me," Marla said before placing her hand over Payton's. "I'm real sorry for what you've had to go through. For what it's worth, I think you are a very strong person."

Another rogue tear slipped out. This time, it was too late to cover.

"Thank you," Payton said with all the sincerity she felt.

"You'll do just fine tomorrow." Granny added her two cents along with a look of solidarity. At her age, she had lived through a whole mess of things, like wars and recessions, and survived to tell about it. One day, Payton would like to pick her brain on how she'd not only survived but kept her sense of humor intact. It was no small miracle.

"Having support from the two of you means more than you could know," Payton responded. The sense of belonging she felt tonight had been something she didn't know to want. She couldn't desire what she hadn't experienced, considering her parents did very little else but fight. Using her as a pawn to get back at each other had been right up there with some of the worst experiences of Payton's life—until the Masked Monster. He made everything leading up to this smaller.

"We're here. Always," they both said in near-perfect unison before patting her hand and heading toward the stairs.

Callum retrieved a laptop along with a pad of paper and a pair of pens. He set them down, and Payton immediately arranged them on the table.

"Where should we start?" he asked.

"Names and addresses of victims," she said, wanting to face the worst part first.

"Okay," he said on a sharp sigh that indicated this was becoming very real for him, too. A person as honest and just as Callum wouldn't be able to fathom what the Masked Monster did to women. His fingers danced across the keyboard. In this moment, she was grateful to be sitting at an angle that made it impossible to see the screen clearly. Instead, she focused all of her attention on the yellow pad of paper as she gripped a pen tightly and clicked.

"First name and most recent victim," he started, "is Sheila Mathers. Nurse." He rattled off an address.

"I don't need to look up that street on a map," she said. "It's two blocks over from mine."

Payton started sketching out her neighborhood while Callum moved on to victim number two.

"Avery Haskel. Waitress," he stated.

"The one who works at the Cracker Barrel in Buddha?" she asked, wondering how she fit in logistically.

Callum rattled off her home address, and Payton drew in a sharp breath. "Two blocks over from the Mathers home."

She made circles on her rudimentary map to mark

the locations. If she was a betting person, she'd go all in the next victim lived in her neighborhood.

"Rochelle Banks, the hotel worker," he stated before punching more keys. He rattled off a third address that was—she'd guessed it—two blocks in the opposite direction of her apartment.

"That leaves Heidi," she said. "Last name?"

"Mortimer," he supplied. "And she's another waitress." He rattled off the name Chili's before outlining her home address.

"We all lived in the same area of town. My place was directly in the center," she noticed. "What about workplaces?"

"Let's check out Sheila's." His fingers tapped the keys on the keyboard. His voice was heavy, and she realized going through the details of the victims was difficult for him, too. It was impossible to detach from the heinous crimes while digging into the facts.

He started rattling off addresses in order. Payton mapped out the workplaces and then positioned the pad of paper so that Callum could see.

"Those are spread out around downtown," she stated as he examined the page.

"Since his targets are in the same neighborhood, my guess is that he's someone who works nearby or your neighborhood is on his commute," he stated.

"Austin's finest must have reached the same conclusion," she said.

"True," he agreed. "It's impossible not to notice all of these crimes are being committed in and around the college campus."

"With a student body of roughly fifty thousand in a small area, he's a needle in a haystack," she concluded.

"Not to mention all the nonstudents who live downtown," he mentioned.

"And the people moving there every week." Needle in a haystack. Even a needle sparkled when the sun struck it just right. All they needed was the right angle.

# *Chapter Eighteen*

"The perp didn't work at your coffee shop," Callum said, thinking out loud. "But that doesn't mean he didn't stop by or work in the same place as one of the victims. He might have followed the first one home and then started noticing others in the area."

Payton nodded.

"Have you looked at the pictures of any of the other victims?" he asked, hating to put her through reliving any of this even though it was necessary.

She shook her head.

"I'd heard something about it. My boss told us all to be careful walking around, especially if we were alone," she said. Her gaze unfocused, like she was looking inside herself for answers, as she'd done once before, or maybe it was her way of detaching enough to be able to talk about it. "But I'd been too busy with work and school to pay much attention."

He covered her hand with his, noticing how small hers was by comparison. Her quiet strength was another in a long list of admirable attributes. His chest squeezed as tension lines appeared on her face, around her eyes and lips—lips that didn't smile nearly often enough. Once this ordeal was over, Callum hoped to change that.

"Speaking of school, I should probably check to see if grades are up," she said.

"Do your profs normally grade essays so fast?" he asked.

"This one promised to since we're at the deadline to drop the class without penalty," she stated.

He minimized the screens he'd been working on and slid the laptop over to her. Not a few seconds later, her fingers danced across the keyboard. She frowned.

"Did you fail?" he asked.

"No, but I barely passed," she stated on a sharp sigh. "I was getting As before this."

"I understand, but no one would blame you for dropping your classes this semester," he said.

She nodded even though her chin came up in defiance.

"Letting him win would be worse than barely passing," she seemed to decide. "I'll keep plowing through, even if I fail. At least I'll know that I've given it my best shot."

"There's no shame in that," he agreed. Payton was a remarkable person and deserved the world. Could he give it to her?

"Since the detective on the case has to be looking at this from the same angle we are, why hasn't he come up with anything?" she asked, repositioning the laptop for him.

"I asked whether or not you'd seen the pictures of his other victims because of the similarities among you," he stated. "All five have long brown hair. Yours has those caramel highlights, which is different, but other than that each has straight hair and bangs."

Payton shivered.

"Creepy," she said in almost a whisper. He couldn't agree more.

"Your face shapes are different, so you're not carbon copies of one another, but this guy obviously has a thing for brunettes," he mentioned.

"All the blondes who live downtown should breathe a little easier," she said.

"He likes attractive women," he continued, though none could hold a candle to Payton's beauty. "Which could mean he was scorned at one time or abused by an attractive mother."

"He had curly black hair," she said.

"That helps narrow our search," he offered even though it didn't rule out a whole lot of folks. "We know we're looking for a male with curly black hair."

"And blue eyes," she said. "They were pale blue."

"Those details cut down the population quite a bit, since we mostly can rule out Hispanic males," he said.

"True," she stated. "Although he could have been wearing contacts, and he might have dyed his hair or had on a convincing wig."

"A wig might explain why the law can't seem to collect DNA evidence on this guy," he reasoned. "So, we might be looking for someone with a shaved head and pale blue eyes."

"It would be easier to glue a good wig to his head," she said, nodding her head. They might be making baby steps, but this was progress. The spark returned to her eyes. He'd never been more convinced that returning to Austin and walking the streets, interviewing friends of the deceased was a good idea. Facing them as the only survivor would be hard for Payton. If there was anything he could do to ease her pain, he'd do it in a heartbeat. Finding this bastard and locking him away would go a long way toward restoring Payton's faith in humanity, not to mention make her feel safe again.

"You're good at sketching," he said, motioning toward the drawing of her neighborhood and the city. "Think you can do that for him?"

"I guess so," she said with a whole mess of uncertainty in her voice.

"It will help to get a sense of height and build and put him back at the forefront of your thoughts," he said, putting a hand up. "I wouldn't ask this of you if I didn't think it could make a huge difference."

She nodded, looking resigned.

"Who knows, maybe if I get him on paper it'll get him out of my head," she said before picking up the pen.

"Can I have the top page?" he asked.

Payton carefully tore it off before handing it over. He studied the page, committing the details to memory as she busied herself with the sketch. Callum moved on to the social media accounts of the deceased and started a document so he could capture

names of those who looked like friends. The nurse
had the least amount of social activity. Sheila had
been in a relationship, but it looked to be new, only
a couple of weeks old at the time of her death. Her
boyfriend might be the best angle, so Callum sent a
DM to request a meeting.

It dawned on him that Austin PD would be moni-
toring these pages as well as the DMs as part of their
murder investigation—a little too late. They would
likely monitor telephone calls if they'd obtained a
warrant or permission. A face-to-face meeting would
work best, so he figured workplaces were a good
place to start.

A dejected guy who wasn't successful with the opposite sex and who needed everyone to know he was
smarter than them. Possibly even show he was more
powerful. Callum typed the thought onto the document as it came to him. Bald? Wears black wig? Cal-
culating. Studies his victims in advance.

The most realistic wigs came from places that
supported cancer patients. Callum pulled up Google
Maps and searched the area surrounding the murders. He came up with two such shops and added
the addresses to the document under the heading of
places to stop by. He glanced at the clock. The shops
closed at six o'clock, and it was quarter to eight. It
would be nice if he could call and get answers, cut
down some of the legwork tomorrow, since this was
a long shot anyway. Except they could take the sketch
if they went in person. Granted, he could snap a picture and see if the managers would take a look. No,

in person would be best. That way, he could see their reactions firsthand.

First, though, they would hit up the employers of the victims. He needed to ask Payton first, but he would like to walk the couple of blocks around her old apartment.

"There," Payton said. She lifted her head and set her pen down. The image staring back at her was the same one that showed up in her nightmares. She was no artist, but it was as close as she could get with her limited abilities and gave at least a general idea of the man they were looking for.

She held up the notepad for Callum to see, and his fists immediately clenched. She wondered if he realized he'd done it. He clenched and released his fingers a couple of times like he was trying to work off tension. His jaw muscle pulsed. Then he took in a deep breath.

"Good," he said. "This is helpful."

"I know it's early, but we should probably try to wind down for the evening," she said, thinking this was as much as she could take for one night. Her brain needed to shut down for a little while.

"That's smart," he agreed. "I'd like to get up around four o'clock to get on the road. The nurse can be our first stop. Based on her social media profile, she worked a nightshift, and I'd like to catch her coworkers before they leave, if possible."

"Okay," she said. Her arms felt like they'd been

wrapped in a soaking-wet blanket. The heavy weight on her chest made it difficult to take in a breath.

Callum stood up and took their coffee cups over to the sink. He rinsed them out and then placed them inside the dishwasher.

"I'll let Atlas out," he said. "Go ahead to the guest room."

"Will you stay the night with me?" she asked, hating the shakiness in her own voice.

"I planned to, as long as it's what you want," he said.

"I do," she said quickly. "It's impossible to think of doing any of this without you."

He nodded before calling to Atlas, who surprisingly got up and followed Callum out the back door.

Payton sat there at the table longer than she probably should have, staring at the sketch. She poked her finger in his face.

"You don't get to take away everything I've worked for," she said to him. Hearing those words and seeing his features solidified her resolve. "I'm coming for you, and you are the one who is going to lose."

Payton didn't know how, why or when, but she committed right then and there to see this thing through until this monster was locked behind bars for the rest of his life. As long as she had air in her lungs, she would continue to track him down. For once, he could feel what it was like to be hunted. She'd been content to let the law do its job. The message in the phone call that had convinced her to go to the capital was clear. He wasn't giving up until she was dead.

She was no longer alone in this fight. *Alone*. The word stuck in the back of her mind. This guy watched the women he intended to murder for days…weeks? Did he purposely pick women who had no family to back them? Women who were single? Payton got up and headed toward the guest room, pad and pens in hand. She figured Callum would bring the laptop.

Four o'clock in the morning would come way too early, and she wanted to be awake and alert for the drive. They could go over what they knew on the two-and-a-half-hour ride to Austin. Based on the map, they would be sticking to the downtown area. They could easily hit all the stops in a few hours. If that turned up no leads, they could wait. This guy had to walk around or through her old neighborhood. It would be so easy for him to slip on a burnt orange UT hoodie and blend in with the crowd. He was average height and slender and could be mistaken for a college student. He *could* be a student for all she knew. The thought she'd passed him in the hallways or while cutting across campus sent another shiver racing down her spine.

Payton set the pad and pens down on the coffee table before heading into the bathroom to shower and brush her teeth. She stood under the warm water for a solid ten minutes before washing up and then facing the mirror over the sink. After brushing her teeth, she joined Callum in the connecting guest room.

"Mind if I use the shower in here?" he asked, holding on to a change of clothes that he'd tucked underneath his arm.

"I'd prefer it," she said with a small smile. They had their work cut out for them tomorrow. Going there to hunt for the monster was risky in so many ways. He might see them first and disappear, even leave the state. He could set up shop somewhere else and murder again. "This end of the house feels a million miles away from everyone else. I can see why it's good for guests. They get a lot of privacy. Too much for me under the circumstances."

He nodded and smiled, but the sentiment didn't reach his eyes as he passed by. He did, however, stop long enough to give her hand a squeeze. The familiar jolt of electricity comforted her. Too quickly, he let go and made his way to the bathroom.

Atlas was curled up on a makeshift dog bed that had been built out of what looked like a couch cushion form another room. He was already snoring and looking snug as a bug in a rug. Seeing him take to Callum warmed her heart. Granny had some kind of magical fairy dust for dogs. *Dog whisperer* wasn't nearly good enough a name for her. Marla seemed to have the touch with animals as well. Then again, Atlas didn't have a problem with females. The progress Callum had made with the dog was nothing short of a miracle.

The bed had been restored. It looked like there was a new comforter and probably sheets on there as well. A water bowl had been set on a tray near Atlas for easy access. Callum's family had thought of everything. She reminded herself not to get too used to having someone around who looked after her and

Atlas. This temporary setup would end soon enough, and she would go back to restoring the house across the street. Atlas would heal, and she would finish school at some point in her life. Money was tight, and she needed to think about starting a business online like she originally thought. Anyone could put up a storefront these days, shop yard sales and then resell online. She could invest in supplies to put a little dazzle on jackets or clothing items. She'd always had a creative side and wanted to do something with it but was always too chicken, going for a practical job instead. Maybe she could use this situation as the push she needed to go for it and leave her comfort zone.

Payton walked over to the coffee table and looked at the tablet again. She picked up the pen and wrote one word: Alone?

The spigot turned off in the next room. Payton climbed underneath the covers after dimming the lights. The king-size bed was big enough for both of them to sleep on without so much as incidental contact.

A couple of minutes later, Callum returned. He started to grab a pillow off the bed.

"You don't have to do that," she said. "I trust you to sleep here, and you'll be more comfortable."

"Are you sure about that?" he asked, and his voice was low, gravelly. "I'll give you the trust part, but I'm not sure sleeping next to you will be more comfortable, considering how much I'll want to hold you."

"Good, because I was about to ask you to do just that," she said. "Hold me."

## Chapter Nineteen

Callum slipped under the covers and met Payton in the middle of the bed. He wrapped an arm around her as she curled her body around his. She tilted her head up and pressed a kiss to his lips. His body tensed as need washed over him like a tide, one muscle at a time.

"Sleep tight," was all he could say after one kiss shot his pulse through to the roof.

"You, too," she said in her sexy, sleepy voice.

They had a long day ahead of them tomorrow. Tonight, he wanted to be her shelter in the storm.

"Callum," she started.

"Yes," he responded.

"Can we leave the lights on dim?" she asked. "Being in a new place can be disorienting. Seeing your face when I first wake up will keep me from panicking."

"Sure thing," he said. He couldn't imagine what she was going through or the trauma that would surely haunt her for years to come. They'd mapped out homes and workplaces. It wasn't much to go on, and he was one hundred percent certain the law had already done the same. Callum's plan was to watch everyone around Payton. If they happened to walk past the Masked Monster, he would have some kind of reaction—a moment of shock, or recognition. He'd called her to come back to Austin. Callum had a feeling the guy had spotted the two of them in the parking lot. He must know that she had a friend now. Speaking of which, Callum needed to take a picture of the sketch and send it to his office in case the perp showed up poking around there. He grabbed his phone and did just that.

While Payton was in the bathroom, he'd committed the sketch to memory, and he was ready for tomorrow.

Leaving the ranch while threats were happening wasn't exactly a warm and fuzzy idea. A few competitor names came to mind in terms of who might want Hayes Cattle to go out of business. Duncan Hayes had been one helluva rancher. He'd built this place up from scratch. Callum's mother had made references to his grandfather's upbringing being tough. She shied away from offering specifics. He figured there were things his grandfather wasn't proud of in his past. Deacon had been tight with Callum's grandfather, and he had a juvenile record. There could be a prison record, too. Deacon was reformed, honest and had been loyal to this family and the ranch for as long as Callum had memories.

Everyone deserved a second chance and, to Callum's thinking, privacy. His mind shifted to the social media pages of the victims. Too much of people's lives was online for anyone to see. Many folks put up pictures of themselves at their favorite hangouts, making stalking or at the very least watching someone easier than it should be.

Callum didn't have a social media account, but Hannah had spent far too much time on hers. She loved taking selfies and posting about their lives. Ironic how unhappy they were as a couple when her social media account made them look enviable. Maybe she'd been trying hard to convince others that they were a good couple so she could persuade herself to stay.

His mind bounced back to the threats on the ranch and the other thing—whatever that was—his mother was keeping from him. Would Deacon have an idea of who was posing a threat? It might just be buzzards circling now that Callum's grandfather was gone. He made a mental note to circle back and speak to the ranch foreman after returning from Austin tomorrow night. Payton's situation was urgent, but so was ranch business. He didn't take threats to his mother lightly.

For the rest of the night, Callum's mind bounced back and forth between the ranch threat and Payton's situation. He could only hope tomorrow would bear fruit.

The alarm on his cell caught him off guard. He hadn't gotten a wink of sleep, and still the hours went by in a blur. He eased away from Payton, figuring he could give her a few more minutes of sleep while he took Atlas outside and made a note about his feeding times and amounts. He ripped a sheet of paper off the pad after turning off his alarm. He unplugged his cell and pocketed the piece of tech. A pen sat next to the pad, so he grabbed that, too, before heading over to Atlas.

Callum took a knee beside the sleeping dog, far enough away not to spook the animal.

"Hey," he said to Atlas, who blinked open his eyes slowly. The pain medication was doing wonders for him in enduring the cone. It most likely took the edge off the annoyance and helped him sleep. He was a brave soul. One who would do a good job of watching over Payton. "Do you want to go outside?"

Atlas's tail wagged, but he didn't budge.

"Okay, go back to sleep," he whispered.

As if on cue, Atlas put his head down and closed his eyes. It was also a huge sign of trust, and Callum's heart responded. The dog had Callum wrapped around his paw with a move like that one.

Callum stood up and then headed down the hall. He could pack a light breakfast and make a couple of to-go cups so they could get on the road quicker. It dawned on him they might want to use a different vehicle today. He could borrow his mother's SUV for a smoother ride anyway. The windows were tinted enough to block an outsider from seeing in too easily. And if the perp saw them in a truck yesterday, he wouldn't be looking for an SUV today.

As he fixed up a lunchbox in the kitchen, he heard footsteps from the hallway. The smell of fresh brew filled the room as he turned to find Payton walking toward him. She walked right up to him and planted a kiss on his lips that made him want to climb back in bed. Until he realized she was half-asleep. Sleep-walking?

"Payton," he said as he snapped his fingers in front of her dazed eyes.

She blinked a couple of times, like she was coming out of a trance. "Oh, hey."

His lips still burned from the kiss, so he regretted that she couldn't feel the same sensations. She probably didn't even remember it. Shame, he thought.

"Good morning," he said with a raspy voice.

"Is that coffee I smell?" she asked before heading straight toward the machine.

"Yes, it is," he confirmed. "Help yourself."

The tasks ahead were going to be taxing for Payton, so he stopped what he was doing, walked over to her and brought her into an embrace. He pressed his lips to hers.

"Whatever else happens today, I want you to know how brave you are," he whispered against her mouth. "And strong."

She tasted minty and like all he needed to wake him up in the mornings, whatever that meant to their relationship. Relationship? Did they have one? They had been quick to shy away from defining what was happening between them. This wasn't the time to figure it out—but soon. Callum needed to decipher what she meant to him, because his heart thundered as she pressed her body flush with his, and he'd never felt an ache in his chest this deep for anyone. Or a hurt so deep at the thought of her walking out of his life.

"So are you," she said right back, causing him to smile despite his serious mood. Only Payton had that effect on him.

"Let's go find this son of a bitch," he said, redirecting his focus before he got lost in her clean, spring flower scent.

"That's a deal," she said with renewed resolve. "First, coffee."

The two worked side by side in the kitchen gathering up supplies and, once again, he was struck by how natural it felt to be together this way.

"I packed food, but we can take time to eat right now if you're hungry," he said.

"I'm good," she answered. "I'd like to get on the road as soon as possible."

He agreed. There was no point in dragging out what they needed to face.

After they coaxed Atlas out to take care of business, Granny joined them in the kitchen. Callum gave her a big hug, and his heart warmed when she did the same to Payton.

"We'll be back by supper if all goes well," he said.

"See you then," Granny said with a wink. "In the meantime, I'll be here hanging out with my boy."

"Do you think Mom will mind if I take her SUV?" he asked, fishing out the keys to his truck and tossing them onto the granite island.

"Why would she?" Granny asked, but it was more statement than question.

Callum grabbed his mother's keys from the hook

by the hallway leading to the garage. "We'll see you soon, then."

He and Payton gathered up the supplies they'd put together. In another touching moment, Payton bent down to Atlas's level, gave him a hug, then whispered what sounded like reassurances into his ear. Atlas rested his head on her hand as she spoke.

When she was done, she pushed up to standing, thanked Granny and followed Callum to the garage and the waiting SUV. They took their seats and positioned the supplies. Callum held up a hand before locating the key to the metal gun cabinet in the garage. He pulled out a Sig Sauer, for its compact size, and a box of ammunition. There was a holster than would allow him to carry the weapon on the waistband of his jeans. He grabbed it and put it on so he could hide the gun.

Back in the SUV, he secured the Sig in a black bag that his mother kept in the back seat. She kept emergency supplies inside, along with a couple of provisions for when she drove to check fencing far from the house. The ammunition box went in alongside it.

Reclaiming his seat, he checked the time before programming the first address into GPS—the hospital.

"Thank you for staying with me last night, Callum. I hope it wasn't too much trouble," she said as he navigated out of the garage, down the long drive and onto the farm road.

"None at all," he said, wishing this was the right

time to tell her how much he wanted to do that every night. "Not even the slightest inconvenience."

"Oh, good. I was worried when I woke up that you might not have been able to sleep because of me," she continued.

He couldn't, and only part of it had to do with her. He wasn't worried, though, because he'd gone days without sleep while tracking dangerous poachers who threatened the herd.

"I'm good," he said, figuring she didn't need to know how long he'd stayed awake going over the details of what needed to happen today.

It was dark outside and would be for hours. This was a special time, when the whole world was quiet. Callum hadn't watched the sunrise in far too long. He didn't give himself much of a break or time off. An epiphany struck him. He'd been focused on the option of having someone run the ranch for them when maybe he should let his second in command at his logistics company step up and run the show. Trust had been shattered when he'd caught Hannah and Trey together, betraying him. But Gregory Brewer had been nothing but honest and on top of running the show while Callum was here. A monthly meeting might be all that was required for Callum to stay involved with his business.

"What do we have to eat?" she asked by the time they made it to the highway.

The next on-ramp would set them on their path to Austin. Before he could answer, he caught sight of a speeding vehicle coming up from behind. For some folks, being awake at four forty-five in the morning might be carryover from the night before. Ranchers might be waking up at this hour and getting started, but Callum had come across enough drunk drivers at this time to know when to get out of the way.

He put on his turn signal and then switched lanes, figuring this guy was in a race to get onto the highway. Fine. So be it. Callum had learned a long time ago to pick his battles. An erratic, speeding driver wasn't someone he wanted coming up from behind.

The vehicle changed lanes, too. *What the...*

Callum focused. He'd been in sticky situations with aggressive drivers before. He slowed down and switched back to his original lane. Not a second passed before the vehicle behind him did the same. A drunk driver was one thing. Something felt off about this. He couldn't get a look at the driver, considering the high beams were on. The odd part was the vehicle should be swerving if there was as a drunk driver behind the wheel. When the driver changed lanes, it had been smooth.

His initial assessment of a drunk driver dissipated.

"Is it him?" Payton asked, checking the side-view mirror.

"I doubt it," he said. "This doesn't seem like something he would do based on the attacks so far. He likes to charm his way inside, make himself think he's cunning. A direct attack doesn't seem like his mode of operation. Not to mention the fact he couldn't possibly have followed us home."

"He might have placed something on the truck," she said.

"True. My guess is that he wouldn't recognize us in my mom's SUV," he reasoned. He could be wrong, of course, but this didn't fit.

"What about an accomplice?" she asked as the vehicle gunned it. The headlights hit high enough for Callum to realize this was some kind of souped-up version of an SUV or truck. His mother's transportation didn't respond in the same way when he hit the gas pedal. It struggled to gain ground and failed to outpace the one behind them.

He shook his head.

"This isn't right" was all he said as he navigated onto the shoulder to allow passage and give this jerk one more chance to divert. There was plenty of room to go right on by. High Beams wasn't having it. They followed like a magnet to steel. This was on purpose. The reason someone might have followed them from the ranch while he was driving his mother's SUV dawned on him. "Whoever is driving that vehicle might be the person threatening the ranch."

Payton brought her hand up to cover a gasp.

"Hold tight, okay?" he said.

"Got it," she responded, bracing herself.

Not a second later, High Beams smacked into Callum's bumper. His head jolted forward, and his arm instinctively reached over to protect Payton from hitting the dashboard. The reality she had on a seat belt wasn't relevant when instinct took over.

Callum muttered a few choice words that he

wouldn't repeat at Sunday church. He cut the wheel a hard left, aiming for the highway, and was cut off by High Beams. The windows were tinted, and he hadn't been home in too long to know any of the players anymore. Plus, this jerk could be an out-of-towner.

High Beams caused him to miss the on-ramp. He was going to get on the highway and what did he think? Callum could outrun him?

"Can you see if there's more than one person in the vehicle?" he asked Payton.

She craned her neck around.

"He's coming at us again," she stated before dropping down into the seat a moment before impact.

Callum bit back a curse.

"Are you all right?" he asked.

"As much as I can be," she stated. "But, yes, I'll be fine."

And then she surprised him by unbuckling.

"What are you doing?" he asked, hitting the brakes.

"Don't do that," she said. "Hit the gas and give me a few minutes."

He did, wondering what she had up her sleeve. A few moments later, she showed her hand, so to speak. She'd loaded the Sig and had it in her hand.

"Do you know what to do with that?" he asked. A gun in the hands of someone inexperienced or untrained was dangerous.

"I've been to a shooting range," she said. "I'm better with a Glock, but this is all we have."

"As long as you know the basics of safety, I'm not

complaining," he admitted as the vehicle roared up behind them. "Buckle in. Quick."

The thought of anything happening to Payton was an absolute gut punch.

She made it in her seat just in time for another hit. Again, they jolted forward. This time, Callum's temper flared.

"If he wants a fight...that's what he'll get," he stated, swinging a wide left before doing the same on the right. High Beams tried to follow, and his tires squealed.

Callum slammed on the brakes, and High Beams followed.

"You loaded the gun, right?" he asked Payton.

"Yes," she said with a tone that said she was mildly annoyed.

"Just checking," he quipped before turning the wheel and slamming on the brakes. "Try to hit his tires."

Payton hit the auto button to roll down the windows and then took aim. She aimed her weapon at the right driver's side tire and squeezed the trigger mechanism. The kickback caused her hands to shake, but she held steady as High Beams must have slammed on the brakes. The sound of tires squealing and then High Beams rolling—the crunch of metal scraping against concrete—filled the otherwise still night air.

Callum brought the SUV to a complete stop before Payton handed over the Sig.

"Good shot, by the way," he said before exiting the vehicle and recommending that she stay put. She didn't, and he shouldn't be surprised that she wouldn't want him out there on his own. If the situation was reversed, he would have done the same.

As High Beams skidded to a stop, Callum approached. He came around to the driver's side. The window was shattered, and pieces of glass were scattered all over. He got a good look at the driver. Anger ripped through him.

"Timothy Gainer," he said. This was a shock. What the hell was he doing here? Callum reached in and jerked the guy he knew from high school out of the driver's seat and onto the hard soil. "Are you threatening my family?"

"This is so much bigger than me," Timothy mumbled as Callum pulled him away from the vehicle. "You have no idea."

Then he lost consciousness.

# Chapter Twenty

The sun was rising by the time emergency crews cleared the scene. Timothy was taken away in an ambulance. Reassurances were given that he would be okay—and also arrested as soon as he was medically cleared. Apparently, Callum knew the guy from way back in high school. Their families weren't exactly besties, but there didn't seem to be a good reason for him to be targeting the ranch, either, according to the statement Callum had given the sheriff's deputy. They would know more when Timothy could speak, which meant he was conscious and could be questioned. From what Deputy Wall could tell, an item from the back seat had smacked him in the back of the head, rendering him unconscious.

Deputy Wall said he would be in contact with Callum and his family as soon as he knew anything.

They might have lost a few hours, but if they'd made headway on the threat toward the ranch, it would be worth the wait. Payton had fallen in love with the Hayes women and wanted whoever was intimidating them to be brought to justice.

Thanks to Callum's quick thinking and excellent driving skills, the SUV was in great condition despite the bumper being rammed several times. It had a few lumps but was perfectly functional. They reclaimed their seats and got back on the road. By the time they made it onto the highway, her stomach growled.

"There's food in the lunchbox," Callum said. "It's been a long morning, and you should eat something."

"I will if you will," she countered, realizing they were in the same boat in the food department.

He shook his head.

"Don't wait for me," he said. "I'm good with this coffee."

"It's long since gone cold," she said. His mind was clearly still on the events with Timothy. "Do you want to talk about what's bothering you?"

"Later," he said. "Right now, I'd like to shift gears and focus on what questions we're going to ask at the hospital."

"I'm thinking we'll go for things like what was Sheila like? Did she have any friends at work? Any enemies? Did anyone seem to have a crush on her?" She rattled the questions off the top of her head.

"I've been thinking about staying on at the ranch for a while," he finally said after a thoughtful pause. "And I do realize that I'm bouncing topics."

"I'm sure your mother would appreciate that," she said. A growing part of her wanted him to stick around, too.

"The ranch needs me," he said. "And I'd like to step into my role there. I never have, because my grandfather was a strong character. He made it known that he didn't need anything or anyone after my father died."

"We all need each other," she said without hesitation. "He probably needed you and your siblings more than he was willing to admit."

"He was one big question mark," Callum stated on a sharp sigh.

"People aren't really that complicated, Callum."

"What does that mean exactly?" Callum asked. There was no irritation in his voice. It was more like curiosity.

"How it sounds," she said. "You mentioned that your grandfather and Deacon go way back."

"That's right," he validated.

"You said that Deacon used to get into trouble with the law. I'm guessing your grandfather knew him from that time period. So, they must have been locked up together," she reasoned.

"That's impossible," Callum said a little too quickly.

"Why?" she asked.

"Because I would have known," he stated.

"Are you sure about that?" she asked. "Your grandfather was distant with you and your siblings, yet he remained close to his son's wife."

"And?"

"It signals there are things in his background that he was too embarrassed to tell you guys," she stated. "Your mother would keep his secrets because she loved him. He's been kind to her over the years. He lost his son. She knew the family secrets, so she would be protective of him because he'd turned his life around."

Callum sat quiet for a long moment, silent, and she worried that she'd crossed a line. None of this was her business, and she certainly didn't want to put her two cents where it wasn't asked for or wanted. Family was sacred, especially to a man like Callum. He might not have gotten along with his grandfather, but she could hear the love and respect in Callum's voice whenever he spoke about Duncan Hayes. There was pain there, too.

"I guess that makes sense," he finally said.

"Or I could be totally wrong," she backpedaled, not wanting to be the one to break the news to him that his grandfather might have a criminal record or burst any bubbles he might have been living in. "It's not my place to make these kinds of assumptions."

"It's probably good to get an outsider's perspective," he said after another long pause. His gaze had narrowed, and she could see that he was concentrating hard on the new information. Seeing if it resonated? Pulling up old memories? Conversations? "I'll give it some thought."

Just like that, a wall came up between them on the subject of his family. Payton understood the topic was closed. Rather than push where she might not be welcomed, she found the lunchbox and then handed Callum an apple before taking one for herself. When those were finished, she moved on to power bars. They were about as tasty as eating dirt and sugar, but they had protein. The bars would sustain them for a while.

Austin traffic lived up to its promise of being brutal. Thankfully, Callum stopped off for coffee, giving her an opportunity to stretch her legs. She didn't want to ask, considering she'd kept quiet for the rest of the ride. She'd given him a whole lot to chew on. He needed time to digest this new information that could change his perception of his grandfather.

Payton sipped the fresh brew, which was nothing like the coffee at the ranch, as they pulled into the hospital parking lot. Callum parked as she finished the last swallow. He exited the driver's side first and came around to open her door for her. She climbed out of the SUV and held tight to his hand as they cut across the lot.

"Do we know what floor she worked on?" Payton asked as they entered the double glass doors of the ER.

"Right here," he said.

The ER lobby was half-full. Kids were sprawled across their mothers' laps, their legs spilling onto the seats next to them. Muffled coughs dotted the room. Concerned mothers stroked their children's hair while comforting them with books or toys. There was half a construction crew around the room, blood and makeshift bandages on various hands or appendages.

Callum strode up to the Plexiglas window. The intake nurse blushed when she looked up from her computer screen. She smiled and shifted the divider over to open one side.

"May I help you?" she asked as her gaze landed on Payton. The woman's muscles stiffened as she made eye contact. The vibe was more than embarrassment at flirting with Callum.

"We're here to talk to someone about Sheila Mathers," he said.

The nurse's expression dropped to sadness, and her eyes never left Payton.

"What do you want to know?" she asked.

Callum leaned in, more than likely to pull her attention away from Payton and back to him. He probably didn't like the focus on her any more than she did. Signs pointed to the woman recognizing Payton from news articles. It made sense folks at the hospital would follow the story.

"Who her friends were and if anyone here had unrequited feelings for her," he said, coming right out with it. They didn't have time to beat around the bush.

"The law came by and asked everyone a whole lot of questions," she confided.

"Oh yeah?" Callum seemed to go along with the flow.

"Yes," she said, leaning forward conspiratorially. "Except the person she was closest to on our shift just got back from vacation yesterday. They didn't speak to her, as far as I know."

"Do you mind giving us her name?" he asked.

"Sure," the nurse said. "Nadine Humphry."

Payton glanced at the nurse's name tag. "Your name is Nadine."

Tears brimmed in green eyes. Nadine blinked a couple of times. She glanced around, looking nervous.

"I might have been closest to Sheila, but we never did anything together outside work," Nadine admitted. "We were coworkers and liked taking breaks together when we could. This place is hopping, and we rarely have downtime."

"Did you speak to the law?" Callum asked.

Nadine shifted in her seat, suddenly looking mighty uncomfortable. She shook her head. "They left messages on my phone for me to contact them when I returned. I was in Cancún, so it's not like I was a suspect."

"I'm afraid you're going to have to fill in some blanks for me, Nadine," Callum started, his voice even.

"I'll try," she said.

"Your closest work buddy is brutally raped and murdered, and you can't be bothered to head straight to the police station when you get back into town?" he asked.

The question seemed to cut hard. Nadine drew her head back like she'd been punched. There was another emotion present, too. Fear?

Payton leaned over the windowsill.

"I can only imagine how difficult this situation has been for you," she said, taking the good-cop role to Callum's bad-cop routine.

"You have no idea," Nadine started, glancing around again.

Payton had been right on with her assessment before. She'd seen fear in Nadine's expression.

"Tell me, then," Payton said. "Help me understand."

"Do you know the coffee shop on Congress Avenue? The one closest to the bridge?" Nadine asked.

"I do," Payton said, realizing it was the one she used to work at.

"Meet me there in half an hour," Nadine said.

"Done." Payton reached for Callum's hand before turning and walking out of the building. She kept her lips zipped until they were back in the relative safety of the SUV. "She knows something, but she's afraid to say what it is."

"How did you figure that out so fast?" he asked.

"The way she looked at me, like she recognized me," she said. "She immediately went stiff."

He nodded.

"By the way," she began. "The coffee shop."

"What about it?" he asked.

"It's where I used to work," she stated.

"Coincidence?" he asked.

"How likely is that?" she replied.

"She might have read about the place in the news after you escaped," he offered. "There was probably more information than anyone should know about you in the articles."

"Privacy is never guaranteed these days," she said. "But that's part of why I kept far away from the news after this all happened. I didn't want to know what was being said about me and my life while I was trying to process what had just happened and how I could have allowed this person into…"

"Believe me when I say that I know all about trusting the wrong person," he said. "Except that it isn't always about trust, and we should be able to believe in one another."

"What you said is true," she said. "I should have trusted me. My instincts that day were telling me to run and not to let this person into my apartment. He ambushed me with kindness when I was having a frustrating moment, and still my gut was telling me not to go along with it. Ignoring it almost cost me my life."

He reached across the seat and clasped their hands. The connection brought a wave of calm over her. Those same instincts said she could trust what was happening between them, even though her brain warned her not to get too close to someone who might move back to Houston, to someone who could shatter her despite the short time they'd known each other.

"We have time to make one more stop before we meet up with Nadine," she said. "I think we should change course."

Callum nodded.

"Are you saying we should go to Sheila's house?" he asked.

"How did you know?" She was curious to know his line of thinking.

"She was his last victim that we know of before you," he pointed out. "He would have gotten better over time. If he was going to make mistakes, it was going to be earlier."

"True," she agreed. "He would become even more meticulous over time and with experience."

"One hundred percent agree," he stated. It was good to realize they were on the same page. "We have to dig deeper."

Going to Sheila's meant heading back to Payton's old neighborhood. Icy fingers gripped her spine as she took in a deep breath, wanting to run as far away as possible. She couldn't, though. It was time to find answers.

"Let's do this," she said to Callum.

# Chapter Twenty-One

Sheila's home was a garden-style town house two blocks from Payton's former apartment. Callum pulled up across the street from the complex and set the engine to idle. The roads were tight in this neighborhood and vehicles lined the streets, giving barely enough room for the SUV to squeeze through.

"We can sit here for a while or go walk around the town house," he said to Payton, who'd gone quiet. The way her eyebrows drew together and her lips compressed, he could tell she was deep in thought.

"I'd like to people watch," she said. "Even though I know the probability of him strolling past right now is next to nil, it's good to get my bearings again."

"We can sit here as long as you like," he said. "No rush and no need to push anything if you're not feeling it."

He couldn't imagine the thoughts that must be rushing around in her mind at being a couple of blocks over from where her life had almost ended. She took off her seat belt and leaned over the console. He wrapped his arm around her and held her tight. She was most likely giving them a reason to sit there, making them look like a couple. And yet it ranked right up there with one of the most intimate moments of his life.

Outside the front windshield, the street was lined with trees. There was a mix of single-family homes, apartments and town houses in the area. The sidewalks had large cracks from the overgrown trees whose branches extended over the street, creating a canopy-like effect.

This street didn't have as much foot traffic as he'd imagined it might. It was solidly midmorning at this point, so morning classes might have the usual occupants on campus.

"Buses run all over town to pick up students. I take the bus most of the time, because it's easier than driving and gets me where I need to go. With a little patience and an ID, you can get pretty much anywhere," Payton said, leaning her head on his shoulder.

"Walkers are big here, too," he said. "If car traffic in Houston is rough, Austin is on steroids."

"My vision of this guy might be totally off, but I'm thinking he's a walker or someone who takes the bus. The university has an extensive network, but there are city buses as well," she reasoned. After a few beats of silence, she said, "You know, I think I'm good sitting in here with the doors locked, if you want to go investigate the town house. Just be careful, because I'm sure nosy neighbors are watching out and possibly the police to see who comes around looking curious about the place."

"That's probably true," he said. "The police's worst nightmare is this guy striking again right underneath their noses."

"Now that you mention it, makes me wonder if he would lie low for a bit," she said. "The heat is on, especially around here."

"Which might make pulling off another killing that much more exciting," he pointed out.

"This guy is sick enough to get a kick out of it," she said. "I think he'd settle for finishing the job with me first. It's something he seems determined to do."

"Not on my watch," Callum ground out.

Payton lifted her face toward him. Her tongue slicked across her lips before he kissed her.

When he pulled back a few moments later after tasting the sweetness there, he said, "I'll be right back."

She nodded, so he slipped out of the driver's seat. He clicked the button on the key fob to lock the doors behind him before heading toward the town house. A quick look back for reassurance helped him refocus. He had no idea what he was looking for at the town house. Similarities to Payton's place as well as the others?

The town house had crime scene tape surrounding it, so he walked on past rather than stop and be obvious about what he was doing there. She had an end unit, so he walked along a winding path that led to a shared pool area and backyard.

Her unit had the blinds closed. There wasn't much to see, and no one was around. Could be the time of the morning, or the seclusion might be one of the reasons the bastard had chosen her. If no one paid attention to someone who walked the path to the pool area, he could have easily watched her. Since her patio could be seen from the pool, he could have stalked her from there. The front door wasn't visible, though. Walking through the front door...*no*, being *invited* through the front door gave this guy a sick charge.

Payton had said she'd been carrying groceries up the stairs. What had Sheila been doing? How had he charmed her into opening the front door and inviting him inside?

This guy worked alone. He would want all the credit. The phone call to Payton could be explained by the guy tricking someone into thinking they were playing a practical joke. Callum wasn't concerned about there being two people involved in setting up the crime.

The perp wasn't stupid. He had an ego. A guy like this would leave some type of trademark. One the law would keep to themselves to stop copycat crimes and ensure any future killings could truly be linked to him. Not knowing what that was put Callum at a distinct disadvantage. He took a deep breath. He wasn't going to get anywhere by standing here near the town house, and his thoughts kept circling back to Payton, alone in the SUV. Even with tinted windows and locked doors, his pulse kicked up a few notches at the thought of her being by herself. At this distance he would hear something: a scream, a gun being fired, a baseball bat taken to a windshield. Still, his heart pounded inside his rib cage.

Making visual contact with the SUV dropped his pulse into a reasonable range. He exhaled the breath he'd been holding on the walk back when he could see the outline of Payton in the passenger seat through the front windshield. She sat back, so it was impossible to see her features clearly. The bright sun contrasted against the dark inside of the SUV.

He reclaimed the driver's seat before clicking on his seat belt.

"Find anything?" she asked.

"She lived in an end unit. Me walking along the pathway right next to her patio that wound its way to the common pool area didn't seem to get any attention," he said.

"Too quiet is as bad as too easy," she observed.

"It seems so," he said before putting the gearshift into Reverse so he could work his way out of this spot.

His back end had barely moved when he heard a police siren. He put the gearshift in Drive so he could wedge into his spot well enough for the law to get past him. With narrow streets and vehicles on both sides, that was no easy feat.

The SUV with lights and sirens roared right up beside them and wedged itself blocking him in. And stopped. An officer came out of the passenger side and around the back of their vehicle.

"Hands where I can see 'em," he demanded in a low, commanding voice.

Payton's hands immediately went up, as did Callum's. He glanced over and noticed the blood had also drained from her face. She just sat there, frozen.

"Driver, put the window down," the cop barked.

With slow, careful movements, Callum brought his left hand down to the button that brought the passenger side window down.

"I need to see some ID," the officer said to Callum. He was bald. A cop would have a whole lot to lose if he was identified as a killer. Based on the sketch, this guy was thicker around the chest area, but his arms didn't reflect it, which mean he had on a vest. Probably Kevlar. The height worked based on Payton's description, but a telltale sign was her reaction to the sound of his voice.

Was this the Masked Monster?

He produced his ID and handed it over as a crowd started to gather on both sidewalks. The cop took the cards in one hand. His right palm sat on the butt of his weapon, ready at a moment's notice.

"Do you mind telling me what this is about, Officer?" Callum asked.

"I'm investigating a suspicious person call," the cop said.

Callum glanced at the name tag on the officer's shirt. "Wickham."

Every muscle in Payton's body seemed to tense up all at once. She breathed out slowly. Something was very wrong with this picture.

"I REMEMBER THAT name from the coffee shop," Payton finally found her voice as the cop moved back to his own vehicle to check Callum's ID. "There was a customer who always gave his last name. Wickham. I always thought it was strange, so it stuck with me."

"You tensed when you heard him speak," Callum said. "I thought it was him."

"It could be, but he's a cop," she admitted. A shiver had raced through her when she'd heard the cop speak. "It's not quite right, though. The cop's voice is deeper, and there's a similar accent that's not quite a twang."

"He might do that on purpose when he's targeting someone," he pointed out, and she'd had the same thought.

As Wickham returned to her side, she tensed. She told herself to relax and not to give him a reason to hold them up any longer. They had a name.

"Can I ask what you folks are doing over here, Mr. Hayes?" he pressed but something passed behind his eyes when he mentioned the last name. Hayeses were legendary in Texas, she realized.

"Yes, sir," Callum stated. "However, I'd like to know what we did wrong before this conversation continues. It's the first thing my lawyer will ask, and I don't want to get chewed out before lunch. You mentioned a suspicious person call. What does that mean, exactly?"

The officer's lips thinned, but he gave a slight nod.

"A neighbor called in a possible Peeping Tom," he admitted.

"Do Peeping Toms usually bring a date along with them?" Callum asked. His question seemed to score a direct hit with the cop. A dirty cop would explain so much. Like how the perp got ahold of her cell phone number. Going back before that, if he worked this beat, that would make it easy to keep an eye on his targets. It seemed bold, but then, this guy was trying to prove he was smarter than everyone else. The question was, why? Why jeopardize his career? Also, didn't cops have to pass psychological tests? Of course, someone with a high IQ could get around them, couldn't they?

She studied the cop's facial features and tried to envision him in a mask. So many emotions shot through her, causing her hands to fist. She couldn't rule him out.

"No, Mr. Hayes, they do not," Officer Wickham relented.

"Good, because I'd hate to bring up this incident with the governor at Thanksgiving in a couple of weeks," Callum said, clearly throwing his weight around.

"Neither one of us wants that, sir," Wickham conceded.

"Then, are we free to go? Because we have somewhere to be," Callum stated calmly. She'd never been prouder to sit next to someone. The cop was not going to get away with bullying them.

"Yes, sir," he said through clenched teeth. "I guess you are."

"I'm going to have to request you move your vehicle, since we're pinned in here," Callum continued, unfazed. "And I need your badge number before we do anything else."

The cop supplied it, and Callum took note.

Payton wanted to clap. A man who'd taken an oath to uphold the law needed to be held to the highest standards. It was probably incredibly rare for a bad egg to get through the system, but she'd witnessed enough news stories to realize that it did happen. Anyone, man or woman, who abused the badge should be treated on par with the common criminals they arrested. She was one hundred percent certain every good cop would agree with that statement wholeheartedly.

Wickham retreated to his vehicle before whipping around them and speeding off.

"I hope Nadine is still at the coffee shop and doesn't think we stood her up," he stated. "I'd also like to do a little digging into Officer Wickham's background. See what kinds of bones we can dig up."

"Agreed. He was too close to the voice not to be suspicious," she said.

"We'll have to figure out a way to get information on him," he said. "In the meantime, maybe Nadine will be able to give us something else to work with or a new direction."

"My instincts are on the cop," she said. "Something very fishy is going on with him."

Callum nodded.

"You know what I think about going on your gut," he stated.

"I know better than to ignore it again—and his voice was familiar," she said.

She wondered why Nadine had been so secretive at the hospital. The intake nurse knew something. There was no question. Would the information help or waste more time—time they didn't have?

## Chapter Twenty-Two

Callum located a spot two blocks over from Coffee, Etc. He opened the parking app on his phone and set them up for an hour. It was probably overkill, considering Nurse Nadine had looked like she was about to jump out of her skin and would probably spook at the slightest noise in the coffee shop. It would give them time in case they had to wait for her.

"Why do you think she wanted to meet at my former employer?" Payton asked. He'd had the same question.

"We're about to find out," he said. "At least, I hope."

He reached for her hand and then linked their fingers. Nadine sat in the corner of the café, where she could watch the door.

"Order two coffees while I go talk to her," Payton said as they entered. "I really don't want to speak to anyone else right now."

"You got it," he stated, letting go of her hand, missing the connection the moment they broke apart. It was probably best if they split up anyway. Plus, this would give Payton a chance to talk to Nadine alone and possibly establish a comradery.

He placed the orders and casually glanced around the café. The cop did bear an undeniable resemblance to the sketch. He'd seemed a little too quick to stop anyone from poking around at the scene of the first crime, which signaled guilt or cover-up. After speaking to the cop, Callum couldn't figure out which one they were dealing with.

What would make a cop look the other way?

Callum thought about his brothers and sisters. He would do almost anything for any one of them. Blood was thicker than water. Any of them could call him up on a moment's notice, and he would drop whatever he was doing to come to their aid.

But there would have to be a compelling reason for him to hide criminal actions. Those went against everything his family stood for. He remembered what Payton had said about his grandfather's possible criminal background. It made sense and would explain a whole lot about the past. It took someone outside the family to point out something that seemed blaringly obvious to him now.

"Cal," the barista at the end of the line said. He'd made it simple for them, cutting his name down to three letters.

As he walked toward the table in the corner, the barista called out the next name.

"Wickham," she said as a man walked out of the bathroom. He immediately turned and headed toward his drink that was now sitting on the counter.

The name caught Payton's attention as well. He hurried over to block Wickham's view of her and the off-duty nurse. The man bore a striking resemblance to the cop.

"Nadine was just telling me that Sheila was secretive about dating a cop," Payton said, keeping her eyes trained on Wickham.

"You don't think?" he asked, figuring he didn't need to spell it out.

"She broke it off and got quiet," Nadine said. "I asked if she was okay, and she would shrug it off. Then she said the cop didn't take it so well and he was following her. She picked up with an old boyfriend to try to give him the hint, but then..." Nadine brought a paper napkin up to blot her eyes. "She never came back to work, and what happened to her was all over the news."

This explained why Nadine was so scared to talk about any of this.

"Why did you pick this coffee shop?" Payton asked. Nadine shrugged.

"She used to have coffee cups from here and I figured it was out of the way," she stated.

Callum turned in time to see the other Wickham lock gazes with Payton. He bolted out the door and onto the street. Callum jumped up out of his seat and followed. The door closed before he could get to it, giving Wickham a head start. It didn't matter much, considering Callum could outsprint the best of them.

Wickham cut across the street. Tires squealed as he bolted, pushing over folks on the teeming sidewalk.

"Excuse me," Callum repeated more times than he could count as he pushed through the crowded sidewalk. He got Wickham in his sights before the other man cut into an alley and pushed his legs until his thighs burned. Taking care to cross the street had put him at a disadvantage, but all those years in track were paying off now.

Callum dived at the backs of Wickham's knees. He folded over backward as Callum nailed the guy. A crack that sounded like bone filled the air as Callum spun around until he was on top and Wickham was on the bottom.

An elbow landed in Callum's chest, causing air to whoosh out of his lungs. Anger shot through him. He grunted and climbed on top of the perp, jamming his knee in the guy's back. Phones came out. A few were aimed at him and the Wickham from the coffee shop. Others seemed to be calling 911.

The thin Wickham tried to wriggle out of Callum's grasp, to no avail.

"Get off me," Wickham said as Callum looked to Payton for confirmation.

"I don't know," she said. "It could be either one."

People gathered in a circle around Callum as he squeezed his thighs a little harder to keep this guy in check.

"Freeze," the familiar cop's voice cut through the gasps of the crowd. Officer Wickham worked this beat. Did he get the call? He would have been close enough to respond. "Put your hands where I can see 'em and step off my cousin."

These two shared the same last name. Were they working together? Callum glanced over at Payton in time to see her reaction to the officer as she locked eyes with him.

"Not a chance," Callum said, anger ripping through him at her realization.

"Hands where I can see 'em *now*," Officer Wickham demanded with greater agitation in his voice.

Callum didn't need to turn around to where the officer was standing to know the man's gun was pointed at the back of his head. The gasps from the crowd said it all.

"I'm not letting a criminal escape," Callum said in as calm a tone as he could muster. "I'd like everyone here to get out your cameras if they aren't already out and record this, because if this cop shoots, it'll be to protect his relative, who is a criminal."

"Donny didn't do anything wrong." The officer repeated the words almost in a mantra, louder each time as he paced.

"Look around," Callum stated. "Because you're being recorded and, this time, your cousin won't get away with rape and murder." He knew full well the officer was the real perp but couldn't say it right then. "You'll never get away with shooting me to keep me quiet. Look around you," Callum said.

A pair of officers on bicycles came riding up. Folks in the crowd started yelling about police brutality.

"What's going on here?" one of the cops asked Officer Wickham. He glanced around frantically before bolting to the left. An officer stepped out of the crowd.

"Whoa there," he said. "I'm going to ask you to put your weapon down. There's no threat here."

"Don't do it, cousin," the Wickham underneath Callum said. "Shoot this bastard. You gave those sluts what they deserved."

"Shut up, Donny," Officer Wickham bit out. Perspiration beaded, dripping down his forehead.

"It's the truth and we both know it," his cousin complained. "That's why I helped you."

One of the other officers stepped forward. "Put the weapon down, Officer. Don't be stupid."

"Don't let him tell you what to do," Donny managed to get out. "Me and you decide who dies. It's just us."

"It's over," Officer Wickham said before setting his gun on the concrete and then lacing his hands behind his head. He seemed to realize he was outgunned and outnumbered.

"This is the Masked Monster," Payton said to one of the officers. "My name is Payton Reinert. He tried to rape and then kill me."

Recognition seemed to dawn as one of the officers placed handcuffs on Officer Wickham. Another came over to arrest Donny. The minute the bastard was in custody, Callum rolled onto his back and tried to catch his breath. Payton was at his side in a heartbeat, while Nadine gave a statement to the police.

"Officer Wickham threatened Nadine not to tell anyone that he'd dated Sheila," Payton explained.

"That's why she was afraid to talk to us in the hospital. Said he might have eyes on the floor where she worked. It was the reason she didn't go to the station to give a statement."

Payton involuntarily shivered as she blinked.

"You're safe," Callum said to her. The news didn't seem to be sinking in as she sat next to him and stared at all the activity going on around them. Statements were being given. Arrests were being made. "He can't hurt you anymore."

Tears streaked her cheeks as she shook her head. "No, he can't."

The last squad car pulled away as Payton sat next to Callum. *It was over.* Those three words were almost impossible to believe. She would be forever changed by the experience, but she would work hard not to let it define her.

"I want to see my dog," she said to Callum.

"Understandable," he said. "I'm sure he misses you."

There was something else she needed to say, and it had to do with her and Callum.

"I went against my instincts once and almost died. I made a promise to myself that I would never make that mistake again," Payton said to him as they stood up. The thought of going back to a life without him was too awful to consider. He might not feel the same, but she needed to tell him what he meant to her. "Those instincts are telling me to trust that what we have going on between us is the real deal and can go the distance. I might not know the little things about you yet, like your favorite color or whether or not you like pizza or a hamburger the best. Isn't that what spending a lifetime together is all about, anyway? Discovering all those little ticks that make a person special?"

Callum's expression gave away nothing of his feelings.

"What I'm saying is that I have fallen hard for you, Callum Hayes," she continued. At this point, she might as well go all in, no matter the cost to her pride if he didn't feel the same. "I love you, and I can't imagine my life without you."

"I never believed in love at first sight until you, Payton," Callum said with the kind of smile that caused her chest to squeeze and half a dozen butterflies to release in her stomach. "I would have laughed if someone had told me that I could know someone on the deepest level without investing a whole lot of time to date. Except that I did that with someone in the past and still didn't know them at all when it came down to it. Whereas with you, in a strange way I feel like we've known each other all our lives."

She held her breath and waited for the scariest word in this situation…*but*.

"I'm head over heels in love with you," he said. She let out a slow breath. "More than that, I'm ready, willing and able to make a lifelong commitment to you right now. I'll move into the farmhouse with you, if you want, because I want you to feel that connection to your family." He took a knee. "But first, I have a question to ask. Your answer doesn't change anything I've said up to this point."

Payton let her happiness spread over her face in the form of a wide smile. Anticipation filled her heart and joy spilled over.

"Would you do me the incredible honor of marrying me when you're ready?" he asked, taking her hand in his.

"Yes," she said without hesitation. "When we're both ready."

She didn't need to overthink the answer. There was no one she'd rather do this life beside. Callum was kind, caring and compassionate. He was intelligent and honest. Even his stubbornness was a positive when applied to the right circumstances. Plus, the man was hotness on a stick, which might not be the most important quality, but it sure didn't hurt. After getting to know him and seeing his character, he only became better-looking. So, no, it wasn't difficult to come up with an answer to his question. "With all my heart and soul, I'd like to marry you, Callum Hayes."

He stood up, picking her up in the process. His embrace was tender but strong. Her feet might have left the ground, but her head was squarely on her shoulders. Nothing in her life had felt as right as this moment, and she had every intention of enjoying it to the fullest. Because the one thing she was absolutely certain of was that life was going to hand her a whole lot of ups and downs, highs and lows, joys and disappointments.

And even during the darkest days of her life, the sun had eventually shone through the brightest.

"Let's go home," she said to the man she was ready to spend the rest of her life with…her home.

## Epilogue

Callum poured two cups of coffee and brought them to the table where Payton was finishing her final essay for the semester. Long, slender fingers danced across the keyboard. She stopped, and a wide smile broke across her face.

"There. Done," she said proudly. "It was a great idea of yours to ask if I could finish my coursework early. Thanksgiving is next week, and my term is over."

"I'm sure you passed everything, too," he said, just as proud of her for sticking it out under the circumstances.

"This semester changed my life," she said. "And we saved others."

"Donny Wickham started chirping like a bird after he was put behind bars," he said, joining her at the table and setting down the pair of mugs. "He asked for a plea bargain to reduce his sentence, since he served as an accomplice."

"Detective Lansing said the Wickham cousins came from a rough upbringing," she said. "Donny's mother used to sexually abuse both of them when they were boys. Elijah Wickham, the officer, used to be forced to spend summers there. He apparently never told his parents, but Lansing said he doubted it would have done any good if he had."

"It's no excuse," Callum said, shaking his head, "but that kind of trauma might explain how Elijah could have snapped."

"Lansing said it also explained why Elijah joined the force. To have authority over others," she said. "They usually ferret out those kinds of prospects early in the process, but Elijah slipped through the cracks."

He nodded.

"I'm guessing Donny's mother had brown hair," he said.

"That's right," she said with a shiver. "And Elijah's victims were all women on his beat, which made it easier to keep watch over them. His cousin works maintenance at the university, so he was a fixture around town as well."

"Hiding in plain sight. All the victims were people they came across in daily life," he said with a head shake. He reached out and touched Payton's hand. "Your victim's statement should get you out of showing up in court to testify later."

"I want to be there," she said. "I want the jury to hear my voice and see my face."

"Then I'll be right there beside you," he said before reaching down to scratch Atlas behind the ears. The dog was on the mend and doing better every day.

"What are you planning to do about Timothy?" she asked, changing the subject on him.

"He's refusing to elaborate on what he said before," he stated. "Charges against him have been filed, but that's all we can do for now. I do, however, plan to get to the bottom of the threat against the ranch."

"You know, we could stick around here and live across the street once the house is done," she offered.

He held up his cell phone. "It's amazing how easy it is to run a business with one of these."

"The last time you spoke to Gregory, he seemed pretty psyched about taking on more responsibility," she pointed out. "Between the ranch, Houston and my great-aunt's home across the street, we'll always have a pillow to lay our heads on."

"I don't care where we sleep as long as you're next to me," he said before leaning over and kissing Payton, his love, his future.

"Good," she said when they pulled back, "because you're stuck with me forever."

"I'm counting on it," he said with a smile.

\* \* \* \* \*

*Look for more books in* USA TODAY *bestselling author Barb Han's new miniseries,*
*The Cowboys of Cider Creek, when*
Riding Shotgun
*goes on sale next month. You'll find it*
*wherever Harlequin Intrigue books are sold!*

# COMING NEXT MONTH FROM

## HARLEQUIN
# INTRIGUE

### #2139 RIDING SHOTGUN
*The Cowboys of Cider Creek* • by Barb Han
Family secrets collide when Emmerson Bennett's search for her birth mother exposes her to the Hayes's cattle ranching dynasty. But Rory Hayes's honor won't allow him to abandon the vulnerable stranger, even when she puts him and his family in the line of fire...

### #2140 CASING THE COPYCAT
*Covert Cowboy Soldiers* • by Nicole Helm
Rancher Dunne Thompson spent his adult life trying to atone for his serial killer grandfather. But redemption comes in the form of mysterious Quinn Peterson and her offer to help him catch a copycat murderer. They make an unexpected and perfect team...until the deadly culprit targets them both.

### #2141 OVER HER DEAD BODY
*Defenders of Battle Mountain* • by Nichole Severn
Targeted by a shooter, single mom Isla Vachs and her daughter are saved by the man responsible for her husband's death. Adan Sergeant's vow of duty won't be shaken by her resentment. But falling for his best friend's widow could be deadly...or the only way they get out alive.

### #2142 WYOMING MOUNTAIN HOSTAGE
*Cowboy State Lawmen* • by Juno Rushdan
Within moments of revealing her pregnancy to her coworker with benefits, FBI Special Agent Becca Hammond is taken hostage. Agent Jake Delgado won't compromise his partner's life—or their unborn child. But will he risk an entire town's safety just to keep them safe?

### #2143 OZARKS MISSING PERSON
*Arkansas Special Agents* • by Maggie Wells
Attorney Matthew Murray's younger sister is missing and Special Agent Grace Reed is determined to find her. But when the case looks more like murder, both are drawn into a web of power and deceit...and dangerous attraction.

### #2144 CRIME SCENE CONNECTION
by Janice Kay Johnson
Journalist Alexa Adams is determined to expose every bad cop in the city. But when danger soon follows, she's forced to trust Lieutenant Matthew Reinert. A man in blue. The enemy. And the only one willing to risk everything to keep her—and her mission—safe from those determined to silence her.

**YOU CAN FIND MORE INFORMATION ON UPCOMING HARLEQUIN TITLES, FREE EXCERPTS AND MORE AT HARLEQUIN.COM.**

HICNM0323